PENGUIN BOOKS

AUGUST IN JULY

Carlo Gébler was born in Dublin in 1954. A graduate of the National Film School, he is a writer and director of films, including *Over Here, Rating Notman* (nominated for an Academy Award) and *Country and Irish*. He has had short stories published in the *Literary Review* and *London Tales*. His first novel, *The Eleventh Summer*, is published in Penguin. Carlo Gébler lives in Maida Vale.

CARLO GÉBLER

August in July

PENGUIN BOOKS

To Virginia

Penguin Books Ltd, 27 Wrights Lane, London W8 5TZ (Publishing and Editorial)
and Harmondsworth, Middlesex, England (Distribution and Warehouse)
Viking Penguin Inc., 40 West 23rd Street, New York, New York 10010, U.S.A.
Penguin Books Australia Ltd, Ringwood, Victoria, Australia
Penguin Books Canada Ltd, 2801 John Street, Markham, Ontario, Canada L3R 1B4
Penguin Books (N.Z.) Ltd, 182–190 Wairau Road, Auckland 10, New Zealand

First published by Hamish Hamilton 1986
Published in Penguin Books 1987

Copyright © Carlo Gébler, 1986
All rights reserved

Printed and bound in Great Britain by
Cox & Wyman Ltd, Reading
Typeset in Palatino

The pages lie finished in front of me. Every evening for the last two months I (or should I say August?) have typed them up from my notebook on my secretary's typewriter. I have been touching the manuscript all evening, re-reading passages at random. Sometimes, while reading, I have been able to remember what I was thinking or feeling at the time of composition.

We move forward in life yet we are always reaching back, trying to get hold of that sense of what we were when we were new to the world. When I was innocent, I wanted to write. But then life began and I became separated from myself. As I grew older the separation grew greater and greater.

My life has been a curious journey. How could I possibly have foreseen how I should be brought back to first principles? But I have been.

There is no solution to the problem of guilt. Nothing washes you clean. I do not understand my life but I have reached a sort of grudging truce with it. I'd like to say I wouldn't have had it any different – and I wouldn't – except for those moments when I nearly chose the silence of death. But if I hadn't come so close to the edge, what would have driven me on?

Death comes in its own time. Why take it any earlier? If you do you'll never find out the end of your story.

December 26th 1980

Whilst I was waiting I went to my bedroom window and looked out. The sky was dirty grey. In the street below a couple walked slowly along. They were both wearing identical woollen hats with heavy red bobbles which swayed like anemones underwater. The hats were white and far too bright for the dark coats in which they had wrapped themselves to keep out the penetrating cold.

After they passed I gazed at the tree which grows in our front garden. The bark was wet and dark and the branches against the sky reminded me of black veins. On the bed I could hear my son, twenty-four years of age, clipping the flex and dropping tiny lengths of plastic-covered wire into a porcelain ashtray. All over London, all over England, all over the Western world, depression was descending like water spreading down a wall from a burst pipe. After the great run up to Christmas lunch, the anti-climax of the afternoon was looming.

'I'm just going to tune it to the first station I can find'. Damian interrupted my thoughts. 'I'll do the proper tuning later.'

The plug went into the socket. I heard a voice saying: 'it won't be a white Christmas or even a white Boxing Day. . . .'

I instantly recognised it as coming from a station which only broadcasts news programmes. I stared into the street at the tarmac glistening with winter damp. The purpose of the clock-radio had been so that I could wake up to music. What was the point of it being tuned to a station which never played any?

'Come on,' Damian said. 'Time to go downstairs.'

I turned away from the window. 'Couldn't you set the tuning now?' I asked. He looked up at me, his grey eyes darkening.

'If I say I'll do it, I will. Only I don't want to do it now.'

'Why not now?' I persisted. 'It would only take a moment or two.'

'Why don't you go ahead? Mother'll be waiting.'

'No I'll wait for you,' I said. 'I prefer to.'

'Suit yourself.' Damian began to gather up the wrapping paper scattered around his feet.

'Thank you for the clock-radio,' I said. 'It's a very nice present. I'm very grateful for it.'

He dropped a handful of polystyrene into the wastepaper basket. I knew my son did not want to be alone with me and that every moment was on sufferance.

'Done,' said Damian.

I bent down and picked up a piece of polystyrene which he had overlooked.

'Fusspot,' he muttered and went towards the door.

He led the way down the stairs. I followed. I stared at the back of his head and the irregular untidy line of hair that lay over his collar.

Suddenly I saw, or it seemed to me that I saw, how he needed care. I wanted to reach out but I didn't. It would only have led to accusations.

Eunice was waiting for us in the living room.

'Still warm,' she said, cupping her hands around the silver coffee pot. A tray rested in front of her on the Coronation stool.

Damian stirred his cup. The brown sugar granules moved on the bottom like pebbles on a beach.

'Why aren't you saying anything?' my wife asked me.

'I'm just sitting here enjoying my coffee,' I replied. 'That's not a crime, is it?'

I stared at the glass case in the fireplace. It is filled with stuffed tits and chaffinches sitting on mossy boughs, all with their heads tilted back and their beaks wide open as if they are in full song. Why couldn't Damian tune the bloody thing properly? It was hardly too much to ask, was it? Anger swept over me and soon the all too familiar feeling of heartburn started up. It was like a hot coal resting between my lungs.

4

I drank back my coffee and put the cup down on the tray. Then I stood up and started to walk towards the door.

'Where are you going?' Eunice called after me

'I'm just going to lie down. I've got a touch of indigestion.' I tapped the middle of my chest.

I went into the room opposite, the room we call 'the study' but which has hardly any books in it, took the notebook with the hand-made paper from the sideboard, which had been Eunice's Christmas present to me, and threw myself down on the sofa. The chintz covering smelt dusty. Why wouldn't Damian bloody do something for me for once? I put one of the cushions under the back of my head and stared gloomily out of the front windows.

It started to grow dark and my anger began to recede. Numbness followed, it always does, the feeling like being cemented up inside.

'Are you all right?'

I turned and looked across the darkened room. Eunice was standing in the doorway, a shape without a face. She was wearing her best suede skirt and a blouse with a bow.

'I'm just having a rest,' I replied.

'We were thinking of having a game of Scrabble,' she said.

'That would be nice.'

'Gosh, it's dark in here.'

Eunice stepped forward and turned on the lamp at the end of the sofa.

I blinked.

'It'll soon be time for a drink,' she continued. 'I could use one of your famous martinis.'

'I'll just gather my thoughts,' I replied, 'and then I'll be in.'

'Okey-dokey.'

Her heels clicked as she walked across the parquet floor.

I turned and looked outside again. Beyond the window the trunk of the elm had become almost indistinguishable from the darkness, and the street lamp in the road was glowing sickly yellow. It had come on without my noticing.

My thoughts ran forward to the evening ahead. We

5

would drink bitter martinis with olives in the bottom from little cold glasses; we would play Scrabble on the old frayed board, its missing letter written on the back of a piece of matchbox; and we would eat the baked potatoes which I could smell in the oven as I lay there, along with dry devilled turkey and a lifeless salad. Then we would say our 'goodnights' and go to bed and that would be the end of it. And we would be happy that another Christmas had been survived.

I opened the notebook and touched the paper. It was thick and porous. There was a faint smell which reminded me of the exercise books of my childhood. I took out the pen from my pocket and wrote on the first page: 'Write something in here on Boxing Day and every day afterwards.' What better way to spend my time in the dead week between Christmas and the New Year?

'August,' Eunice called. 'Would you fetch a lemon?'

I left the study and headed for the kitchen.

And that is how I come to be writing this, instead of watching the musical with Ginger Rogers and Fred Astaire. It's playing on the television even as I write. Eunice and Damian are cooing with pleasure from it, this Boxing Day afternoon, 1980.

1981:
Morning

I awoke abruptly. The duvet was lying across my body, and my feet were cold. I lifted the covers back over myself and wriggled my toes. I would lie there until they warmed up. High heels scuffed in the distance, like a needle on the centre of a record, then faded into silence. I thought of my journey to work through wooded streets; of the underground in the early morning haunted by smells of dust and perfume; and of women on the escalators in summer dresses with little red marks on the backs of their ankles where their shoes rubbed.

Summer brought with it a feeling of optimism. Anything was possible, it seemed, except that I knew it was not.

The electric alarm started to whine from the chest of drawers near the door. It was seven-thirty.

I threw back the covers and stepped onto the carpet, furry on the soles of my feet. The room was hot although the window was open, and my mouth was dry. I looked at the gleaming white cupboard doors with shining brass handles, the enormous chest of drawers with the black and gold eagle inkstand resting on top, the full-length mirror decorated at each corner with Greek urns. I felt boxed in by it all, but I said nothing about it to Eunice. Candour would only lead to a row.

'. . . on the A40 it's very bad owing to building works at Northolt . . .' crowed a voice. 'And with one day to go to the Royal Wedding. . . .'

I squinted at Damian's Christmas gift. The tuning band with its thin lines of red was lit up by a green light and the time was announced in calendar letters. I wondered why my son had not re-tuned it for me. Then I remembered Damian was coming at six because it was a Tuesday and decided I would ask him then. I did not like the idea as my son was moody and I could imagine what might happen. Damian's eyes might darken. His mouth might shrink. He might accuse me of always nagging. But I would ask him none the less.

After pulling on my dressing gown I sat down on the spare bed, the one beside my own, the one that had been Eunice's and was still hers if she ever wanted it (but she never did), and found my slippers underneath. They were brown with crêpe soles. From time to time they gave out a peculiar odour like a wet dog and I would have to sprinkle them with eau de cologne even though I knew it evaporated in minutes. 'Uhh,' I muttered out loud when I remembered. It was the day of Harold's farewell lunch. Despite the young man having been asked to leave, the proper niceties were being observed. In my opinion Harold was unstable and I could well imagine a row, pints of lager being poured on my or my partner David's head, and threats of physical violence. When one of the secretaries had been seen off at a similar occasion she had taken off her blouse, climbed under the table and tried to do up everyone's shoelaces. The memory of the past and the thought of the future together made me wince.

I padded out into the hall. I could hear my wife's electric alarm whining behind her door. Eunice always set it to come on early in the morning.

I pushed open her door.

'It's seven-thirty,' I said.

Eunice's face was hidden by the duvet. All I could see was her hair fanned out on the pillow. Nearby her gollywog sat splayed on a chair, limbs like stuffed sausages and dark staring eyes, the guardian of her nights.

There was something sticking out from under her bed. I picked it up. 'Mrs E. Slemic,' I read. 'Two nightly as required. Nembutal.'

'It's seven-thirty.'

Startled, she sat up in bed.

'Oh no, I meant to get up early.'

'That's what you say every morning.'

'Damn!'

Eunice threw herself back on her pillow.

'I've got so much to do,' she said.

'Do you want a cup of tea?' I asked.

Eunice lifted her head from the pillow fractionally.

'Oh yes. Eunice would love a cup of tea. And August, could I have the paper?'

I went downstairs. Her newspaper lay on the brown door mat. I would buy mine later. I objected to paying the newsagent his delivery fee. I stepped across and opened the door. The milk was in the corner beside the indicator pointing at 'Two Pints Please'. I pushed down the silver top of one of the bottles and brought the cold circle of glass to my lips. Suddenly I was back in the kitchen at home in Warsaw, drinking cream from the ladle which Rita was holding to my mouth.

'Where's my paper?' Eunice called down.

'Coming.'

I ran my tongue round my mouth. My teeth felt chalky.

In the kitchen I plugged in the kettle and put Eunice's special blue cup on her special blue tray. Then I went back upstairs and handed my wife her paper.

'Thank you,' Eunice said.

'A pleasure.'

'Do you want to know your stars?'

'Not particularly,' I replied.

'Leo,' she began. 'A good day for business transactions or for large sales such as your house.'

'Oh good.'

'It'll be your birthday soon. How old will you be? I can never remember.'

'Sixty-one.'

'Sixty-one of course. Do you know what you want?'

'Certainly not a set of saucepans.'

Her cheeks appeared to flicker as they always did when she was hurt.

'I didn't mean it like that. They were very nice. But I'm not really the cook, am I?'

Eunice plumped up her pillow and settled back.

'What I mean is, there isn't anything I really want,' I continued. 'Honestly. I don't want you to go to any trouble or expense.'

I left her reading and went out. Dark cupboards lined

11

the bathroom corridor, one with its doors hanging open. The rails inside were packed with Eunice's clothes, their bright colours reminding me of plumage.

I shifted the hangers on the rail inside and slammed the doors. But the cupboard was so full they would not shut.

'Why don't you get rid of some of these clothes?' I shouted to Eunice.

'What are you complaining about now? There's nothing wrong with my clothes.'

'I can't shut the doors because of them.'

'Don't be ridiculous. I shut them every day. Listen to this: "Taurus. You've been a bit down in the dumps recently so why not give yourself a treat? Father, get yourself that lawn-mower you've always wanted. And mother, get him to buy you that new dress." '

I went into the bathroom and noticed a strong smell of antiseptic. Then I saw a bottle of mouthwash standing open on the shelf.

I picked it up and tipped the end towards a glass. I expected the mouthwash to come out in cautious drips but instead a huge spurt of candy-floss-coloured liquid poured out, drenching everywhere. I looked at the top and saw that the dispenser which controlled the flow was not in place. Closer examination revealed it lying in the bottom of the bottle.

'I've just had a disaster with the mouthwash,' I shouted.

'Be careful. The plastic bit fell in when I used it last night,' Eunice shouted back.

I took the lump of dry cloth from the S-bend and began to wipe everything off.

'What about a raincoat for your birthday?' continued Eunice. 'The summer sales are coming up.'

Five minutes later I left the bathroom, my skin shining from my shave.

'Where's my cup of tea?' Eunice called. 'She's getting thirsty.'

She was sitting up in bed, her glasses on her nose, and the carefully folded newspaper resting on her hunched-up knees.

'Result of volcanic eruption. First letter "P". Thirteen letters?' she said.

My mind was a blank.

'Petrification,' she said suddenly, snapping her fingers.

'I'm no good at crosswords,' I said. 'I don't have the right sort of mind.'

'What's that meant to mean? The right sort of mind is abnormal?'

'I don't have a tidy mind is what I mean.'

'You know sometimes you make confusions where none exist. To do the crossword all you need is a modest grasp of English and some common sense.'

'It's not even eight o'clock and you've started.'

'I haven't started anything. Just trying to hold an ordinary conversation, that's all. I mean, if we can't hold a conversation after twenty-five years of marriage, what can we do?'

'I could name one thing that we could do.'

'Oh don't start that again,' replied Eunice without looking up.

'I don't understand you. Disagreement is one of the most exciting things in life. People sparking off each other. That's how ideas arise.'

Faintly, I could hear the lid of the kettle bobbing up and down.

'I'll make the tea,' I said.

'Oh, good August to make the tea. Good to his Eunice. Don't put in too little milk but don't put too much in either.'

I began to descend the stairs. The banister was slippery under my palm. There was an ugly lunch coming and this was how the day started.

'Don't worry, your tea'll be just as you like it,' I called back.

I shut our front door and stood still. There was a faraway sound inside the house. That would be Eunice getting up, I thought. She always stayed in bed until I left. Then she got up straight away, ran her bath and got herself ready for work in half an hour. Eunice worked short-days book-keeping for a small firm of theatrical agents in the West End.

I descended the stone steps and skirted our tiny lawn. It was worn through at the edges to the colour of pigeon. I pulled open our gate and stepped onto the pavement. Two boys in djellabas and a little girl in silk pantaloons chased past me, shouting and screaming. They were followed by a woman in black, the whites of her eyes staring menacingly from behind the mask over her face. I started walking. I heard Arabic, guttural in the distance. Apart from those behind me the street was empty. I stopped in front of the gravel driveway of the house at the end of my road and bent forward to look into the garden. Cemented onto the low wall was a black memorial plaque with white lettering. 'Naughty Puss. Died Boxing Day 1914. He was only a cat but he did his best.'

Every morning on the way to work I read the words 'He was only a cat but he did his best'. They were ludicrous and confirmed what I had heard about the absurd love which the English are said to have for their animals; yet at the same time they summed up for me (which they had gradually come to do over the years) the idea of trying one's hardest even if one was not going to win.

As a child I had had certain spots which I always had to touch on the way to school: the pipe behind the stove which rattled when the wind blew down the chimney; the curving wall at the end of our street; the iron fence near the tram stop; and I thought of this as in no way different. It was a lucky talisman which brought protection every time it was acknowledged. In a long line of magic places this had been my longest-serving and was the most important to me. I even harboured an obscure wish to be buried alongside the puss who had tried his best.

I imagine that as soon as she heard the front door shut Eunice sprang out of bed. She went straight to the bathroom and began to run her bath. I had cleaned the sink after shaving and had carefully folded the towel with which I had dried myself. The bottle of mouthwash was back in its place on top of the medicine cupboard. She noticed my orderliness with irritation and wished that sometimes I could be a little more like other human beings. Then she took off her nightdress, threw it carelessly on the floor and looked at herself in the mirror. She was not delighted with what she saw but then she reminded herself that it could be worse.

When she had finished in the bathroom Eunice returned to her bedroom. So that the seams would not move, she sprayed the back of her legs with nail-varnish remover and then selected a pair of black stockings from her bottom drawer.

I was in the Goldhawk Road. I made my way past a garage with a long-haired Alsatian lying outside in the sun, passed under a railway bridge just as a Hammersmith-bound train was rattling overhead and turned into the forecourt of the underground station.

I went over to the newspaper stand in the corner. There was a woman in front of me in the queue. Her neck was pale with three moles arranged in the shape of a triangle. The vendor handed her a folded newspaper and took her money like a dancer executing a faultless movement. She moved off. I put my hand into my pocket and took out my change.

'Just a second', said the vendor as I was about to ask for what I wanted.

'Morning Jimmie,' I heard a voice booming behind me.

'Hello Mr Buchanan,' replied Jimmie. 'Yours is on the bench inside.'

Mr Buchanan brushed past me and stepped into the booth.

'Should be near the top,' shouted the vendor.

I stared at Mr Buchanan as he leafed through the small pile of newspapers; his thin grey hair was unusually long and curled over the back of his collar. He was wearing a Prince of Wales check jacket and his shoes were gleaming with polish.

Mr Buchanan straightened up and re-emerged holding a copy of *Sporting Life*.

15

'How are you today, Jimmie?' he asked loudly.

'Mustn't grumble, Mr Buchanan.'

I stared gloomily into the booth. On the walls glossy magazines hung from clothes pegs with naked girls on the fronts. The change had grown hot in my palm.

Mr Buchanan was moving off. 'Lady Lavery's Boy,' he said. 'You won't forget?'

I glared at Jimmie. This was really too much. I coughed to emphasise my annoyance and saw that the old vendor's nose was covered with blackheads like tics.

'I'll expect a drink if you have a win,' Mr Buchanan called over the roof of his Rover. Then he smoothed his hair, and disappeared through an open door.

'Yes, guv,' said Jimmie to me in an apologetic tone.

I pointed at what I wanted and handed over my money. I felt irked. Why was my newspaper not left folded for me every morning? I had certainly been a customer for just as long as Mr Buchanan.

Walking into the dark entrance of Stamford Brook I remembered the porter from our apartment block where I had lived as a child. A cheery man, he had been on first name terms with most of the residents. Yet to me, who had lived there for eighteen years, he barely ever spoke, except when he thanked me for the statutory Christmas present which I presented to him annually.

As I waited at the ticket kiosk, shuffling forward every now and again, I reflected gloomily that some had a knack for forming relationships with those with whom they had little in common, whilst others did not. The hall porter had apparently been a lesson to me which I had failed to learn.

The man immediately in front of me set his canvas bag down on the ground and bent towards the glass.

'Willesden Green please,' the man said. 'Is that near Cricklewood?' I watched the man handing a pound through.

The pale green ticket came back.

'I don't know,' replied the shape behind the glass.

The man picked up his ticket and began to turn away. His face was long with deep creases running down from the nose. Suddenly there was a sound of money being rapped on glass.

16

'Ohi,' bellowed the ticket seller. 'You forgot your change.'

The man turned back and slid the coins from where they lay.

'Willesden Green, you've no idea if it's near Cricklewood?' he repeated. 'I'm tuning a lady's piano out there and she said it was near Cricklewood.'

'I told you I don't know,' said the ticket seller.

'Yes it is,' I called out to the man. One of the few benefits I had gained from my job was a wide knowledge of London geography.

'Oh thank you,' replied the man.

I moved forward to the vacant place and looked at the ticket seller through the glass. He was young, in his twenties, unshaven, with bright eyes set close together. There was something porcine about him.

'You know what I wonder?' said the ticket seller, looking straight at me.

I shook my head. Out of the corner of my eye I noticed – which I had failed to notice before – that the man with the bag was tapping his way towards the trains with a white stick.

'What I wonder is, why don't they buy a bloody map?' continued the ticket seller.

'Baker Street please,' I said.

I took my ticket and paid for it without saying anything and went down to the platform. There were schoolboys chasing one another by the vending machine and young men in suits reading tabloids. I looked at the rails and the greasy stones between the sleepers and suddenly remembered what I had been dreaming just before I woke up.

I was in a cave. It was dark and yet I was able to see. The walls were granite and there were huge boulders strewn everywhere.

I took a few tentative steps. Stalagmites and stalactites rose and fell around me. Some ended with a point in mid-air whilst others had joined to form strange pillars. Green slime spread down the walls.

I touched a stalagmite. It was cold and wet and filled with reptilian associations. There was a sound of running water. I looked down and saw a pool spreading in front of me. At one end, where the water flowed in, the surface

17

rippled, but at the other it had a quality of flatness like mercury.

It was then I saw the fish lying suspended in the water. It was the length of my forearm with a thick tapering body and off-white coloured skin. On either side of the head, where there should have been eyes, there were bulges shaped like flying saucers. Above the mouth long black whiskers: the faintest brush and they would sting.

I felt a sense of peace coming over me. Now that I had arrived in the centre of the earth, I had to learn to wait and listen.

The fish began to move, swinging its tail from side to side. With its slow ungainly movements it reminded me of a tin toy.

As it crossed the pool I wondered if it was going to lift its head out of the water when it reached my feet, and speak? But it nosed into a hole at the side and disappeared from sight.

There was a sudden silence. I noticed that the water at the other end of the pool had stopped pouring in. The surface gradually grew stiller and stiller and simultaneously I began to feel a sense of grief and sadness. At first it was a small feeling but it grew bigger and bigger, swelling my body like a monstrous bubble until I felt it was going to explode. It was then that I had woken up. . . .

I began to walk down the platform towards the red signal. I had once seen a television programme about the fish that I had dreamt about. They lived in caves deep in the ground, somewhere in Persia, I thought. Stunned by the film lights the specimens had swum in nervous circles or hidden churlishly in the shade of overhanging rocks.

'These animals are perfectly adapted to their environment,' the commentator had said at one point. This had stuck in my mind, whilst everything else I had forgotten.

The underground train pulled up. I climbed into a smoking compartment as I was more likely to find a seat there.

I turned off Marylebone High Street and headed for

Slemic and Co. on the next corner. I had been making the journey to my business premises for nearly thirty years, and there was no step along the way between the underground and my door which I did not know. The worn coal-hole covers were dark round pupils watching my every move, and the railings of the mansion blocks were peeling candles.

Drawing nearer to the office, I saw there was someone already inside. It was Emma, the secretary and receptionist. She was cleaning with a purple feather duster. I watched her moving, framed by the two 'For Sale' notices. I very much liked Emma: she was quiet and gentle and when she looked at me with her brown eyes I always felt that she was saying 'I understand'. From time to time, when we were alone, we would have tea in my office and we would talk shyly. Emma had told me that her husband was a gambler who had more or less reformed and now worked as a carpet layer. She wanted to have children but for some reason they could not. I had told her that I was married with one son with whom I did not really get on. I had also hinted that my marriage to Eunice was unsatisfactory, hoping to elicit a similar admission from Emma.

Sometimes when she came to work in the mornings, Emma was puffy-eyed, as if she had been crying, and once she had arrived with a swollen lip and two huge black eyes hidden behind ridiculous sunglasses. She explained that she had fallen down the stairs. That evening Emma's husband, who was called Brad, turned up unexpectedly to collect his wife. He smelt of aftershave and carried a bunch of roses. His muscles bulged out of his cheese-cloth shirt showing the tattoos on his swarthy forearms. His kindnesses towards his wife were inept, which was confirmation, if any were needed, of what he had done. And when he was introduced to me, hearing that I spoke with a faint middle European accent, he immediately said, '*Parlez-vous français,*' in a cockney accent.

I opened the door into the outer office. It smelt of photocopying fluid and the Windolene which Emma was spraying onto the dusty base of her anglepoise. 'Hello, August,' she said. Although I had been encouraging her to use my Christian name for years, she never managed to say it without making it sound like a surname.

'Good morning. What are you doing?'

'I'm spring-cleaning. I know it's July but "Better late than never as they say". I feel ever so cheerful today. It must be the Royal Wedding. Are you looking forward to it?'

'I haven't thought about it,' I said. Emma suddenly looked slightly let down, so I added, 'Of course I'm looking forward to it. It's just that I'm not going to let anyone know I am. It's a bit unseemly; old men like me getting enthusiastic.'

'You're only as old as you feel,' she said.

'I suppose you're right.'

I glanced into the other part of the outer office and saw that the desks of Harold and the other junior, Dennis, were unoccupied, and that the door of the accounts office was shut.

'No one in yet? We the first?' I spoke softly and looked closely at her. It was the best way to get across something of what I felt.

'Harold was in but went out.' The springs of the lamp pinged as she ran the duster up and down. 'I didn't see him, but that mangy old baseball coat of his was here when I came in this morning.'

Harold in at the crack of dawn on his last day. What could he possibly have been doing?

'I'm surprised that Harold turned up at all today,' I remarked.

'Oh, he likes his free beer and his free lunch too much. He isn't going to miss them. God, aren't I a bitch? Miaow!'

'Of course you're not. Don't be ridiculous.'

'You always say the nicest things, don't you?' said Emma smiling at me. 'Would you like some coffee? I'm just going to put the percolator on.'

I said that I would and went towards my office. The baseball coat was lying across Harold's cluttered desk, a symbol of him that made me anxious. A number of images passed through my mind. Harold in the same baseball jacket and running shoes, coming into the office with a very properly dressed Belgian banker whom he had just shown around a house. The banker had not been impressed by Harold or his attire. Harold with both his broken wrists encased in plaster of Paris as white as icing-sugar, smirking and saying how a pretty lady client would have to help him when nature called. Harold on the telephone saying jokily to a buyer that no, they couldn't have the house they wanted because it had fallen down from dry rot.

My partner, David, had overheard the conversation and summoned Harold to the office.

'We're here to sell houses not to tell jokes,' David had begun.

Harold had shrugged his shoulders.

'Why don't you wear a suit?'

Harold had shrugged again.

When the interview was over David had described Harold as 'a mealy-mouthed little wanker'. 'And I'm going to have him' he had continued.

After that David had started complaining about Harold to everyone else in the office and making out that his mistakes were much worse than they actually were. 'That boy Harold is a wally,' I once heard my partner confiding. 'I can't sleep at night thinking about the cock-ups that male model is making.' 'Blame it on Harold' had gradually become the catchphrase with everyone until at last it seemed perfectly natural to ask him to go. To my shame, I had acquiesced even though I had not had any reason to dislike Harold in the beginning. Of the two, of course, Harold or David, it was my partner I needed the most.

I passed through my doorway, sat down at my desk and began to open my mail. Mortgage details, house enquiries and unrequested glossy booklets smelling of methylated spirits. In the early days letters had been a source of excitement. But now they bored me and, as I sorted through, my concentration was the lowest I could get away with. If the letter advertised a company or a commodity, out it went; if there was a personal signature, I kept it.

'Mr Slemic? Excuse me.'

I looked up and saw Harold was standing in front of me.

'What is it?' I asked.

21

I had managed to avoid Harold all month, and now here he was in my office. Was he going to make a scene?

'I've got a problem,' Harold said.

He held up a bunch of keys.

'I went to that shop in the Parade in Maida Vale thinking these were the right keys, but they weren't.'

'Why don't you fetch the right ones?'

'I can't.'

'What do you mean, you can't?'

'Because I can't.'

He put the keys down on my desk. His thinning fair hair was swept back and flicked up over the collar like a young girl's. He was wearing a tee-shirt with the word 'Muscle' on the front. He looked stringy and unhealthy inside his clothes.

'Let's go and find them,' I said resignedly.

Heading towards the door I glanced surreptitiously at my watch. It was ten to nine and David did not usually arrive until quarter past, which was a relief. I did not want to be seen by my partner with the first junior we had ever asked to leave, especially if we were fussing around with keys.

I passed the door of the accounts office now with an adding machine clattering away inside, and stopped in front of the half-hidden cupboard where we kept the keys. Harold stopped behind me.

I pulled open the door. The bunches were usually hung inside on hooks shaped like question marks, but all the hooks were bare. I saw at once that all the keys were lying on the bottom. I extracted a bunch and discovered the identifying tag had been removed. It was the same story with the second and the third set. I looked at the cluster which Harold had given me; it was the same story again.

'All the tags are gone,' I said.

'I know. They were like this when I came in this morning. I picked what I thought was the bunch by memory but they weren't they.'

I looked into Harold's face. His beard was thin and I could see the pimpled skin and the outline of his weak chin underneath.

'I really got egg on my face this morning, Mr Slemic, I

22

can tell you.' He continued. 'I had an eight-thirty appointment with that lot and they weren't very pleased when I couldn't open up.'

I looked round, and saw that Harold was pointing at a group of Sikhs sitting in their coloured turbans in a circle around Emma's desk.

'And how do you explain that the tags have been removed?'

'I don't know. It's a mystery.'

'You came in here this morning and they'd just vanished?'

'Are you accusing me, Mr Slemic?' The young man's watery blue eyes were strangely impenetrable.

'How do you think it happened?' I pressed.

'I've no idea,' he replied coldly. 'I'm just reporting the facts as I know them.'

I looked away again. Harold's denials were so adamant they could only have been rehearsed. I wanted to shout: 'How do you think you can get away with a pathetic lie like this?'

I heard one of the Sikhs laughing and remembered the faces of my school teachers, staring sadly out of windows after some lie had been told, or some act of cruelty denied. As a schoolboy, when I had watched them, I had always wondered what they felt like? Later in life the question had been answered and now it was being answered again. It felt terrible.

Suddenly certainty came to me. I put my hand into the pile and pulled out a bunch with a key which was sticking up, the end of which looked like the beak of a bird. A quick check of the serial numbers against the details in the file confirmed that my intuition was right.

I jigged the keys in my hands a couple of times like a heavy stone, whilst Harold stood in front of me with a vacant expression and an outstretched palm.

'These are they,' I said. 'Apologise to them profusely.'

'Yes, Mr Slemic.'

Harold took the keys. I watched him as he crossed the room.

The Sikhs were now at the far end clustered around the giant map of London. They were running their fingers along the coloured pieces of thread which joined up 'For Sale' details with the actual locations.

'I'm most terribly sorry,' I heard Harold saying to them. 'But we seem to have sorted the problem out now.'

The door opened and the sounds of the street roared in, rocking the cardboard display boards in the side windows. Harold smiled at the last of the Sikhs as they filed past him. Another apology was murmured, then Harold sidled out and shut the door.

It was quiet again. As I began to hang the bunches randomly on hooks I was pleased I had kept quiet. If I had challenged Harold, or let him know that I thought he had played a dirty trick, all the anger which he had stored up concerning his dismissal would have been unleashed. There would have been an ugly scene. I also knew that my exasperation was the confirmation Harold had been seeking and to withhold it was the only weapon I had.

I finished rehanging the keys. Some of the bunches swayed gently and even clanged against one another. They reminded me of bats hanging upside down. I decided I would not tell David about what had happened. My partner was the sort of man who would call Harold in and grill him like a headmaster until he got what he believed to be the truth. On Harold's last day that would hardly do. I slowly shut the cupboard door. The keys would have to be sorted out, of course. The afternoon would be a fine time for that. The day before the Royal Wedding, we were hardly going to be run off our feet. All over London, all over England, minds would be focused on buying crates of lager, checking television aerials, and re-positioning sofas. No one was going to buy a house or a flat. And I would get Emma to help me.

I looked across the room at her. She was copy-typing something with an expression of concentration which was almost farcical, in between looking up every ten seconds to see how the coffee percolator was progressing. Yes, she would help me. It would be a pleasant afternoon diversion.

There was a movement behind me.

'Hello, August Slemic,' chirped a voice.

I turned round and saw that it was Doris coming out

24

of the accounts office. Her curly hair was dyed black. She wore red liipstick and the mole on her cheek was painted with kohl. She had once explained herself and the way she looked to me by saying that she was 'a child of the forties'. 'I was born the first day of the decade, Jan first nineteen forty,' she had added.

'Hello, Doris.'

'Isn't it a nice day?'

She moved very quickly to the photostatting machine, lifted the rubber flap and laid out a piece of paper. With a touch of a manicured finger, the machine began to whirr.

'Yes it is very nice,' I said, 'but I always find the summer makes people bad-tempered, don't you?'

I remembered the ticket seller and his rudeness to the blind man asking the way.

'Probably the heat. We're not used to it,' said Doris. 'My dad was in Egypt during the war and I think it sent him barmy.'

'Good morning,' I called through the open door of the accounts office to the girl sitting behind the desk inside. It was Maureen who was plump and came from Fife.

'Hello,' she said, looking up from her calculator.

On the wall over her head there was a grubby poster of a monkey on a lavatory with lavatory paper wrapped around him. I read the caption, 'No job is done until the paperwork is finished,' and slipped back into my office.

I pushed the mailing list of those to whom we sent our 'For Sale' details into the corner of my desk and opened the type script marked 'Houses and Flats for Sale. August Proofs'.

'Abard Rd, 23,' I read, but could go no further. It was half past nine and I was already bored.

I picked up my coffee cup and crossed toward the window which ran along the wall in front of my desk, dominating the room. 'Slemic and Co.' was written across the glass in big gold letters. Beyond the double glazing, all day, every day, the world passed in an endless silent stream, a perpetual dumb show.

I stopped and let my eye wander along the street towards Marylebone High Street. It was filled with traffic and pedestrians; movement lacking any detail.

I took a sip of coffee. It tasted flat and metallic. A woman coming in the opposite direction caught my attention. She was middle-aged with a round face and blonde hair that came straight down to her shoulders. Her small dachshund ran in front of her on a lead, a blue bow around its neck. She crossed the road and stopped in front of the shop opposite my office. Mannequins in bright clothes stared back at her through the glass. She bent down and gathered up her dog. He wriggled in her arms and I could imagine the animal's pink tongue touching her face. As she turned towards the entrance to the shop, I sensed my own office door scraping open behind me.

'Morning. to you squire,' said the voice of my partner.

'Good morning to you, David,' I replied.

Inside the shop the woman I had been watching was now a shadow.

I turned from the window. David was standing in the door with his head twisted over his shoulder.

'Emma,' he shouted.

Her typewriter stopped clacking. 'Yes.'

'Can I have a cup of coffee? I'm absolutely parched.'

'Yes, Mr Humphreys,' came her faint reply.

David half-closed the door.

'Penny for your thoughts,' he said.

'I haven't any,' I replied. 'It's a blank up here.'

I pointed towards my forehead.

'At my age you can get along for hours on end without thinking about anything at all,' I continued.

David dropped his head forming a double chin and looked at me.

'I thought I glimpsed something rather tasty going into "Caprice",' he said, waving towards the shop on the other side of the road, 'and I half-fancied you were watching her with your beady little eyes.'

I began to move towards my desk.

'Did you have wicked thoughts, my son?' interrogated David in a mock-Irish priestly accent.

'Actually I was wondering if she worked,' I replied. This was the truth.

David released the catches on his attache case and opened it. Inside the lid I saw the coloured pens, which David was never without, lined up in a row. They were held in place with something like an elasticated armband. Neat though I am, this neatness of David's always annoyed me.

'Is it two sugars, Mr Humphreys?' Emma's voice wafted through the door.

'That stupid girl,' he muttered. 'Yes. Two.'

'Do you want another, Mr Slemic?'

I stared at the pale liquid in my cup, the colour of sodden cardboard.

'Why not?' I shouted back as I settled into my chair.

Emma appeared from behind on my right. She was wearing a grey dress with buttons up the back. I looked at her as she walked towards my partner. She had longish hair, falling over her shoulders, that was neither blonde nor brown, and a slight but attractive figure.

'Thank you, Emma,' said David without looking up. He was taking something out of his attache case. Whenever she was around, I noticed, David always made a point of appearing to be busy with something.

Emma turned towards me holding the other cup.

'How are you today?' I asked. 'I didn't ask properly when I came in.'

I looked up at her. Her large blue-rimmed spectacles were resting on her nose, her brown eyes magnified behind them. It was a sight which I always found both sad and ridiculous.

'Oh I'm very well, thank you,' she said, and smiled.

She was pretty, I thought, and if she did not wear her glasses she would be prettier.

'Well that's good,' I said.

She turned and walked towards the door, sliding her bangles up her arm as she went.

The door shut. David got up from behind his desk and began to pace up and down.

'Do you notice anything different about me this morning?' he asked.

I looked at the familiar figure of my partner. He was tall but lightly built, with narrow shoulders and thin bones.

27

He was wearing pumps without heels which laced at the side. I found their dandified effect slightly repulsive.

'No,' I said. 'I don't notice anything different about you at all.'

'Nothing.' David turned on the spot.

I looked carefully. The brown striped suit was familiar. The spiky hair was the same length. The face was pale as always, with red eyelids and long black lashes where yellow particles of sleep often collected.

'No,' I repeated. 'You seem just the same.'

David stopped moving and looked at me across the room.

'I think you should be the first person to know,' he said.

He rubbed his hands as if warming them, one of his characteristic gestures.

'It won't come as any surprise to you,' he said, 'that myself and Mrs Humphreys haven't been getting along for some time.'

'Yes.'

'Well, to make a long story short, we're getting divorced. At least, the last bulletin as of one o'clock this morning is that we are. Communication wasn't terribly clear at the time. I was halfway down the street and she was shouting from the bedroom window.'

'Oh dear,' I said, looking away towards the street. Through the blur of people and the vehicles outside, I saw the women in the white dress emerging from 'Caprice'. She was holding a large carrier. As the shop door closed behind her she squatted down and the dachshund leapt from her arms onto the pavement.

I turned my gaze towards David. My partner was playing with a magnet and a paper clip.

'Do you remember Karen?' he asked.

An impression formed in my mind. A woman with long dark crinkled hair and a chin that jutted out.

'You met her at our Christmas party,' I heard David saying.

I remembered being in David's kitchen; it smelt of cloves. A huge pan of mulled wine simmered on the gas, with purple woadlike stains around the edges and a ladle sticking out of the top. Karen was in front of me leaning against the refrigerator.

'I used to act,' she said. 'At university. Amateur productions but they were very good. We toured to Brussels once. I was full of high hopes in those days. Now I'm just a mother with two grown sons and a part-time job as a doctor's receptionist.'

'It's never too late to go back,' I said.

Karen shrugged her shoulders. Her face was very white with ruddy marks underneath the skin. I noticed she had almost no eyelashes.

'It is too late,' she said. 'There are some things, once you lose them, that you can never find again.'

'Such as?' I asked.

'Such as your talent,' she replied, 'if you have any. Scott Fitzgerald for example. He had it and he lost it.'

I was not in a position to argue as I knew nothing about the man she was talking about except that he was a writer. In the doorway a young man pulled a woman under the mistletoe hanging above. They kissed, giggling and laughing. I let my eyes roam over their slim bodies and then, before they would have a chance to detect me, raised my glance upwards, as if that was where my interest lay. The white puff berries reminded me of candlewax. I took a drink of the tepid mulled wine from the thick glass I was holding. Sweet on the tongue, its aftertaste was bitter.

'I would have thought,' I said, 'that parts of the character – such as the part that's talented – only go away if you want them to.'

'Well you think wrong,' she said.

She turned away with a shrug to face the refrigerator. Crackers exploded in the next room, accompanied by shrieks of laughter.

'Look at that,' Karen exclaimed abruptly.

She pulled a piece of paper from behind a magnetised banana that was stuck to the refrigerator door.

'Isn't my best friend Mrs David Humphreys just the last word in efficiency?' said Karen.

I saw the paper was covered with neat rounded writing. 'Two lbs butter, Peas, Potatoes. . . .'

29

'Tomorrow's shopping list already drawn up and dated,' said Karen.

Next door someone had drawn a whistle in their cracker and was blowing it loudly. I took another drink of my mulled wine.

'But what is it they say?' Karen tossed her hair over her shoulder and turned to look at me. 'The most efficient wives are always the dullest! Isn't that what they always say?'

Now it was my turn to shrug my shoulders.

'I don't know,' I said. 'I don't know what they say.'

I held up my empty glass.

'I have to get a drink,' I said.

The memory passed in a moment. 'Yes, I remember meeting Karen at that Christmas party,' I said.

'Well she's what they call the co-respondent in the legal profession, or what you and I would know as the other woman.'

His wife, plain little Midge, might have been dull but at least she had normal emotions. I remembered how once she had cried in public after she had had an argument with one of her sons. The other woman was cold and she gave me an unpleasant feeling.

Beyond the gold letters of Slemic and Co. a window cleaner swaggered by, a filthy rag swinging from the end of his ladder.

'Karen and I have been seeing one another for years', David started. 'At first it was just casual but then it turned into something more serious.'

How ordinary, I thought. How unsurprising.

'Last night Midge and I were having one of our rows,' David went on, 'and I suddenly found myself blabbing it out. I suppose it was inevitable.'

There was a pause. I pictured David's house: the kitchen with its big pine table and the brown cork board covered with photographs of the children; the living room with the imitation coal fire that was really gas and the beaten copper flue; and the overheated bathroom which always smelt of the bath salts which they kept in tall spaghetti jars on the window ledge. In the middle of the setting floated Midge. I saw her with her arms wrapped around herself, and her small pointed nose red from

30

crying, exactly as she had been after the argument with her son.

'What happened after Midge shouted along the street?' I asked.

'I went to Karen's. Her husband's away. Very convenient. She wants us to marry.'

His speech was very quiet as if he were talking to himself.

'This morning she cooked me breakfast,' he continued. 'It was a very strange sensation, I can tell you, sitting in another kitchen with another woman. I want to marry her, too.'

'Why don't you take the day off?' I suggested.

'Good God, no. That would be a disaster. I'd only think about Midge and then I'd start feeling guilty.'

David walked across and picked up the mailing list of those who would receive the 'For Sale' notices.

'What I've got to do is some work,' he continued. 'I'll check through these.' He waved the papers. 'Otherwise I'll go crackers.'

He dropped back into his chair.

Outside everything was out of focus. I could not decide whether I felt annoyed or depressed. Here were two lives – mine and my partner's – but they seemed to be going in opposite directions. My life was unhappy and I was trapped in it, whilst David's story seemed to be the reverse. Why was it my blasted fate, I wondered, to be the one who ended up in the slime and the mud at the bottom of the river? Why couldn't I be the one who floated on the top like a daddy-long legs with legs outstretched, balanced perfectly on the smooth glassy surface?

'You've put a line through Mrs Dubois,' said David loudly.

'Frankly I don't think she's going to buy anything from us. She swans around one house after the other but she's never made a serious offer. I don't think she's got anything to do, except get estate agents to show her around houses.'

'Oh go on. Let's have her back,' coaxed David. 'For my sake.'

His thin lips curled back in a smile, revealing small white teeth.

'Why?' I asked. My thoughts were still at the river: insects buzzing on the surface, the still brown mud below.

'I have a life long fantasy,' said David, smiling, 'and I think Mrs Dubois is the one to bring it true. I'm going to bring her over to the Arab place, invite her to test the softness of the master bed, and hope that one thing leads to another. It's not often you become a free man at my age. I intend to make the best of it.'

He bent his head down again.

I felt a wave of envy mixed with anger. Where were the freedoms and excitements of my life? More than anything in the conversation so far, the remark brought home to me my age. I was twenty years older than David.

'Burrows-Goulding,' my partner muttered. 'Absolutely. Strike them off the list at once.'

I had to act more and think less. Life was not over for me, if I could only change. The problem, as I saw it, was my unapproachable, unyielding quality, which put everyone off. I had to soften. I had only to break the hardness which I imagined as encasing me and I would become a light and aerial creature – nothing as common as a daddy-longlegs, but a dragonfly – now floating on the surface, and now darting through the reeds along the riverbank. I picked up my pen and told myself that as of that day, that hour, that minute, I would have to start.

I imagine that, mid-morning, David slipped out to a telephone kiosk and called Karen.

'How did August take the news?' she asked.

'He's a cold fish, you know,' replied David. 'He just asked me if I wanted the day off. He didn't comment.'

'My husband is coming home tonight,' she said. 'I'm going to tell him.'

'I love you,' he said.

'I love you too,' she replied.

December 28th 1980

Today is Sunday. Of all the Sundays in the year, this Christmas one must surely be the longest and the dreariest. The house is empty. Eunice and Damian have gone to a neighbour's for drinks. I escaped by saying I had to prepare a few things for work tomorrow. I'm a hopeless liar; I was lucky to get away with it.

Outside the long window which looks out at the front, a woman glides along the damp pavement, her shoulders thrown back, her hips thrust forward. A small boy and an Irish setter with its ribs showing are crossing the road and thin wreaths of breath curl from their mouths.

I feel as though I am in a rock. I am a tiny living spirit like a flame encased in it. I long to break through the rock but I can't. Trapped in the darkness my spirit shouts feebly and dreams of some cataclysmic event which, like a bolt of lightning, will shatter the rock and allow the spirit to escape into the light green world that is outside. I dream of this bolt of lightning in many guises. I dream of it in terms of a love affair; of enormous success with my business; of being able to say to people things I have always wanted to say but have never had the courage to say. But it never comes and from this there is only one conclusion to be drawn. The bolt of lightning must come from within. If we want to escape from our prison we must be our own Zeus. Yet which of us has the courage? Not I. I do not want to leave the inside of my rock. Dry, arid, dark; it is also safe, well known, protective.

So there I am locked up in the rock. It is getting steadily thicker. Layer after layer is accreting to it. But where do these layers come from ? My rising sign is Cancer and that is the clue. I am really a crustacean. I am really an organism living inside a shell. I have made my own prison and the making of it is an inescapable fact of my nature. In order to make a passage through life we must protect ourselves. Yet the shell prevents us enjoying what we've been protecting ourselves to enjoy in the first place. If I think like this for very long it gives me a headache.

The old year is going. The new year is coming. Our thoughts turn back and look forward. We make resolves. We will eat less. We will be kinder to our wives. We will stop smoking. My resolution is that I am going to take this notebook which Eunice gave me for Christmas, this notebook which already has several pages filled with my small, crabbed, black handwriting, and I am going to go on writing until every page is covered. Self-understanding is the key to any sort of self-improvement.

After the great rush of words on Boxing Day I came in here yesterday, Saturday, expecting more of the same. I turned on the electric fire and sat down. This notebook lay open in front of me for some time. Then I made my first hesitant jotting. When I read it back it made me wince. I sharpened my pencil. In the chimney flue the wind was howling. My second piece of writing was worse than my first and the third when it came worse again. I was seized with despair as I began to wonder if there is a point in life after which self-expression becomes impossible. I tore out what I had written and threw it away.

I decided I would write the story about the prisoner in the cell which I have been thinking about for a long time. I began to make a list of the events in my notebook. I got halfway and stopped. I was uncertain of the end. I sat back in my chair and pondered various solutions. None of them seemed right to me. It was getting dark outside. I looked at my watch. I had been there for two hours.

When I was a schoolboy I was always writing: little tales, anecdotes, whatever came to mind. They used to call me the 'Scribbler' at home. Then I came to England and, once I had the language mastered, I began jotting again. This was in the RAF. I kept a diary. I wrote short stories. I even harboured foolish hopes about getting something published. But for many reasons nothing ever came of it all.

Eunice and Damian came back a few minutes ago, and Eunice has gone down to the kitchen. I can hear the Magimix. I imagine the glass container filled with fruit or vegetables; the whirring blades; the cutting of the solids into liquid.

Pictures of my family stand on the mantelpiece. There is a black and white photograph of my father. He is in a suit and sports an extraordinary moustache, and he stares straight into the lens. He used to call this his 'rabbit expression'. The portrait of my mother beside him shows just her head and shoulders. Her face and neck are smooth, white and serene like alabaster. She was not like this in life of course; she was temperamental and moody. At the end stands a picture of my brother with his wide moon face. He is aged four. He is standing on a chair wearing knickerbockers and holding his favourite ball under his arm. His hair had been wet for the occasion and, plastered down, it glistens like a wet bathing hat. How well I remember the day the photographer came to our apartment in Warsaw, mother holding my brother under the tap and the way he shouted, 'Hey mother, the water's running down the back of my neck. . . .'

The photographs were sent to me after the war ended by a distant relative. By that time my father and my brother had followed my mother to the grave. They both died of TB. With them dead I had no reason to return.

I am writing at a lacquered desk on which flowers have been painted. I bought it years ago because it reminded me of the folk art of my country. Of course I never saw any folk art when I was there and, if I had, I would probably have despised it. We were a progressive family; our furniture was solid, heavy, up to date. But then I left and came to England and the idea which everybody had of my country in England gradually seeped into me. I forgot the streets of Warsaw humming with trams, the clanging of their bells, the sound of the wheels roaring on the tracks. I forgot our apartment block with its doorman in braid and its lift with a gold-edged mirror and a red velvet seat just like at the theatre. I forgot our apartment with its telephone, its electric light, its flushing water closet. Instead I remembered horses and carts ambling along straight roads across flat landscapes; congregations kneeling outside churches; and little girls in white dresses hurrying through the evening along country lanes towards their first communion – immaculate white dresses of intricately stitched lace, white stockings that hung loosely at their knees and ankles, and veils like the muslin we covered our butter with in the summer. I remembered evenings in a small provincial town (it must have been the town where we went for our summer holidays), a small band playing waltzes, peasants sitting around, the men in suits trying to look like city folk and the women in patterned blouses and coloured skirts; and in the middle a cackling crone with no teeth, weaving around drunkenly, winking at the men and lifting her skirt to the knees as she issued her racy invitations.

Yes, it was a shame that I forgot what I knew and fell in love with the other view of Poland, this Poland of peasants with walrus moustaches, steaming cabbage and green verdure. But all is not lost, for now I am beginning to remember properly again. The scales are dropping away from my eyes, you could say. These rural images which came from the holidays we took are moving to the edge of my memory, and long-forgotten images of the town where I really spent my childhood are once again taking up their proper place in the foreground.

I was four or five. It was Christmas time. I was with my nanny Rita, my little mittened hand held firmly in hers. We hurried through dark streets. A tram rushed by, sparks flying off its wheels. They were golden coloured sparks which lit up the darkness.

We turned into a butcher's. It was the first time I had ever been in a butcher's. Everywhere there were big pink carcasses of pork with shiny skins. They hung upside down from silver rails as if they were racing towards the centre of the earth, galloping towards the hot molten ball in the middle which my father had told me about at great length. In the window were the heads of the pigs, their

36

eyes like wet liquorice; their trotters too, dainty and elegant in comparison to the enormous bulk of the carcasses; and lastly their tails, like little twists of sausage.

'Ugh,' I said, pointing towards them. 'I don't like those.'

Rita looked down at me. 'Don't you like those, darling?' she asked. I shook my head. At the back of the butcher's a young boy in a blood-spattered overall was singeing a chicken over a gas flame. The stubs of the feathers were crackling like burning bracken and I could smell the peculiar, unforgettable smell. 'There's nothing to be frightened of, darling,' Rita continued. 'Those are Chinaman's pigtails.' 'No, they're not,' I shouted. I began to scuff the sawdust on the floor with my booted foot. 'Those aren't Chinamen's pigtails,' I said. 'Those are pee-pees.' 'Of course they're not. Don't be ridiculous,' said Rita. 'Those are pigtails. Stop being silly.'

She asked for what she wanted. As I stood waiting I raked the sawdust, turning up bits of fallen meat or gristle and then covering them over again. It was the sort of game I might have played on a beach, except that it had a grotesque fascination for me which no afternoon in the sand would ever have had. 'Come on darling,' Rita had a package wrapped in white paper held tightly under her arm. A fat man stood over the block chopping away and I saw that where the blade fell the wood dipped down like a worn step.

She took my mittened hand again and we went out into the freezing darkness. 'You know, darling,' she said, 'when you grow up you'll understand all sorts of things which at the moment you're too young to understand. You might think pig's tails are frightening now, but when you're older you'll see that they're not. Do you understand what I mean?' I nodded my head as if I did. She squeezed my hand tightly and we hurried on. My cheekbones started to ache from the cold. There was ice on the ground and once or twice, as we made our way home, we nearly slipped.

When I was in second or third grade, I used to stand

outside the kitchen door staring at the varnished wood, the worn black handle, the brass plate, and listen to mother and Rita as they talked inside. I wasn't interested in what they were saying. It was the sound that fascinated me: the rise and fall of their voices. Then, when I heard one or the other of them coming, I would dart into my bedroom and stand listening to the footfalls of whoever it was out in the hall with my heart beating and pressing against my ribs. I had escaped detection and the excitement was intoxicating.

I remember the darkness, the lumpiness of the cinema seat, the taste of chocolate in my mouth, sweet and cloying; Rita beside me, her face silvery from the images on the screen; empty rows stretching away from us – it was an afternoon matinée; the pianist at the side, his head twisted round at an odd angle so that he could look up; on the screen a tombstone in a fog-filled graveyard at the dead of night; the pianist raising his hands and then crashing them down on the keyboard; my shivering in anticipation that something terrifying was about to happen; Rita squeezing my hand with perspiring fingertips; the slightly musky smell of her scent in the darkness; another crash from the piano; a hand coming over the top of the gravestone, a hand with long and dangerous nails; the top of a head and then a woman appearing with wild unkempt hair and a white shroud falling loosely from her shoulders; another crash on the piano; flashes of lightning darting across the night sky; the adam's apple of the wild woman vibrating; throughout the graveyard, movement under the heaps of earth in front of the tombstones; the earth parting; ghouls flowing out with white, insubstantial bodies; a dance tune starting up; the ghouls linking hands and starting to dance around the graveyard, a huge circle of them, swirling round and round, faster and faster. . . .

My uncle Peter lived in a tree-lined street of villas; his

was squat with a wall that went all the way around it. In this wall there was a big green door beside a stirrup on the end of a piece of wire which was attached to the bell. My brother and I used to take it in turns to pull it. On this Sunday let us say it was my brother's turn. Faraway we heard it tinkling inside the house, the tinkle drifting across the garden. As we stood waiting our mother tidied us; she brushed our hair flat with her gloved hand, straightened our neckties and our spotless wing collars, and removed flecks of dirt from our lapels. When she had finished with us she opened her cologne bottle and dabbed it on her wrists and behind her ears. The smell of cologne, the dust of the street and the smell of tree sap all mingled, unforgettable and extraordinarily evocative for me to this day. Beyond the gate we heard the quick small steps of the maid treading across the paving flags in patent leather boots. The little door behind the grille opened. The maid smiled through. My mother smiled back. 'Good morning, Mrs Slemic,' the maid said. 'Good morning, Maya,' my mother replied. The gate creaked back. Maya was a peasant woman with a wide face and green eyes. Her hips were wide and her skirts used to go straight down from them rather than falling naturally. We filed through. The front garden was small, paved with slabs which smelt of slime and snail. On one side were double gates and on the other the ornamental cherry trees. In May the slimy paving stones would be carpeted white with their blossom.

The house was a low two-storey building, with steps in the middle leading up to the front door and green-painted shutters over the windows. As we walked across the garden our uncle came out of the front door. On Sundays – as opposed to the rest of the week when he worked in a bank and therefore had to wear a frock coat and a top hat – on Sundays my uncle wore a light-coloured tweed suit with leather bindings around the cuffs and patches on the elbows, and underneath a beige-coloured waistcoat. 'Welcome. Welcome. A thousand times welcome,' he shouted to us. He was a big man with a florid face and prone to sweating. He pulled out the large red handkerchief which he always wore in his breast pocket and wiped his brick-red forehead with it. We reached the foot of the steps. 'Well my dears, my dears,' he said, the handkerchief going back in his pocket, 'I won't come down as I know you're coming up.' 'No, don't come down,' my mother said. We began to climb. The banisters were metal and always cold, no matter how hot it was. At the top, beyond the front door and its shining brass knocker, I glimpsed the big mahogany table which stood just inside, the silver letter tray and ivory letter-opener that lay on the top, and the living room at the far end with its big windows opening onto the back garden. It was like looking down a tunnel and seeing light glimmering in the distance. Then our uncle shook hands with us and ruffled our hair which had just been so carefully laid in place by our mother, and as he did so he said, 'Boys of their age shouldn't look too neat, you know. They should look a bit wild. They'll have to spend the rest of their lives dressed up like stuffed penguins so they might as well enjoy their freedom now.' My mother smiled and said, 'Ah, but they look so sweet dressed up as little gentlemen.' Then my uncle turned to her, lifted her gloved hand to his lips and looked into her eyes. 'My dear,' he said, 'you never change in any way except you get lovelier and lovelier.' My mother smiled and touched her hair or her earrings. Nothing further was said. My uncle motioned with his fat hands and we stepped into the villa.

In our first moments inside the hall, because we had stepped from light into dark, our eyes went momentarily blind. Then our sight came back. On our right stretched the stairs covered with red turkey carpet which led to the water closet smelling of carbolic and his bedrooms with their large beds. There was also a strong smell of wax, of cigars, and of something masculine that was unmistakable and unidentifiable. Our uncle lived alone.

Behind us we heard the thump of Maya shutting the front door. My brother and I surged forward like the eight- and ten-year-olds that we were (I being the elder), taking care not to slip on the Persian rug laid carefully on the polished parquet floor.

The living room at the end was large and spacious, with pictures on the walls of Japanese figures, a fireplace with a curved mantle and a glass conservatory leading off it with the round dining table already laid up. I looked through the door and saw the heavy silver, the white plates with gold around the rims, small glasses like egg cups for vodka, bigger glasses on stems for the hock, buckets with ice already floating inside, squares of beetroot, sweet smelling pickled herring, smoked salmon floating in lemon juice, and sometimes small dishes of grey sturgeon.

French windows opened onto the lawn. My brother and I stepped out. The turf was soft and luxuriant underfoot. Roses grew in beds at the side, with pale, recently shed petals on the earth around them, and sunflowers at the bottom, heads nodding on thick stems. In one corner there was a tool shed which smelt of creosote and string and something musty which I connected with earwigs and armadillo-grey woodlice, and in the other corner towered an oak with dark green leaves, a swing hanging from one of its sturdy branches. We stopped, looked around for a moment, assured ourselves that everything was as we had left it on the Sunday before when we had visited, and then ran forward to the badminton net which was always left set up for us in the middle of the lawn.

After lunch my brother was put to sleep on the sofa in the living room: he was not only younger than myself but more prone to exhaustion than I was. My mother and uncle went to sit in the garden under the oak tree and sip iced tea tasting of mint and cinnamon, and I was left to my own devices. I crept upstairs and looked down on them through the lavatory window, and heard the clink of mother's spoon against the glass as she stirred it drifting across the afternoon. After a while I became bored so I went round to the front of the house and loitered in the shade by the gate, eating an apple and a stolen candied fruit. Maya upstairs came to a window (her window?) and waved down to me. Later she came out in her everyday clothes rather than her uniform and talked with me for a few minutes before she went off to afternoon mass. After she left I was alone again and I lingered for hours staring at the villa. The front door was a dark green I have never seen anywhere else. On either side there were two windows with heavy tasselled drapes hanging behind them. These were the windows of the front rooms, the parlour and dining room, where we were not allowed. On the first floor there was a line of five windows with more drapes behind them and shutters at their sides, thrown open and held in place with clasps. The lower halves of the shutters were slatted but the upper parts were solid with a heart cut into them reminding me of the gingerbread house in one of my fairytale books. The roof was gently sloping. Along the edges and the top it was covered with dull-coloured lead and, on one side, odd and out of character, there was a weathercock sitting on top of a globe. It was a still summer's afternoon and I was as still as that metal weather vane until the unmistakable sounds of activity started up within the house – my mother calling for me, my uncle playing an arpeggio on the piano, and my brother's piping cries of 'August, August'. As soon as I heard these sounds, a sense of depression descended, and I rose a little sullenly, skirted the mock cherry trees, and slunk down the passage at the side where the sickly-sweet smell of refuse lingered. Arriving at the conservatory I found tea waiting on a white cloth now slightly crumpled and stained from lunch – dishes of jam, horn-shaped pastries filled with insipid-tasting custard, a type of cake that was black and sour, and chocolates with a crystal in the shape of a violet stuck into the top. We sat down. The adults drank vodka; my brother and I ate our cakes, getting jam between our fingers and caster sugar on our chins; and then, as the shadows lengthened across the lawn, and pools of shade formed under the oak tree, we departed to catch our tram. An hour later, after a bumpy journey which left us feeling rattled, and with church bells sounding across the city, the key was turned by my mother in our front door, and we stepped into our long, dark, carpeted apartment, with its window ledges which were always grimy even though they were washed daily, its corner cupboards in every room which smelt vaguely of gas, and its pipes which knocked together when the kitchen taps were run. As always, father was waiting for us and as always he asked the same question. 'And how was uncle Peter?' he said. 'Same as ever,' my mother said.

Such were our summer Sundays throughout my childhood; and our winter ones were not much different except that we couldn't play outside.

We took our evening meals in the gloomy dining room. Father would sit at one end opposite mother at the other. I would sit opposite Misha. Little would be said and all I would hear would be the sound of cutlery on porcelain, their chewing, my own chewing. A great gulf of silence seemed to stretch between all of us, particularly between mother and father. I connected (quite rightly now that I look back) the tenseness and estrangement to a half-seen and little understood event which I had witnessed at my uncle Peter's on one of those summer afternoons.

Thinking that it would speed up the ordeal, I often ate my food too quickly. I would swallow it without chewing properly and it would promptly stop somewhere in my throat. I would experience something like suffocation for a moment or two and then the heartburn would start, and I would push my plate away and sit back in my chair. Sometimes I took some water but that rarely did any good. 'Are you all right, August?' my mother would ask when she saw that I was not eating. I would shake my head or touch my chest. 'Eating too fast,' she would observe. 'Yes, eating too fast,' my brother piped. 'Enough of that, Misha,' she would say. I would stare at my plate or at the salt and pepper cruet and the little mustard dish that had blue glass inside. At the same time I would touch the tassels that ran along the edge of the table-cloth where they touched my legs under the table. I particularly liked dragging them through my fingers. Being fine and silken they passed through very quickly, almost like sand. After a while the heartburn went, the sensation of its disappearing like a sliding and opening in the chest all at once. I connect these meals and my heartburn, more than any other experience I had, to the state of adolescence.

When I was eighteen I finished school but my further education had not yet been settled. I left home and took

43

rooms, supported by a small income left to me by a deceased relative. I told my parents that I intended to use my free time to study whilst I waited to see how my university applications fared. I did go into the Warsaw library most days, but it wasn't serious. I didn't have to be there at a certain time, my work wasn't in any way supervised, and I didn't have the pressure of examinations hanging over me.

After some weeks of this I met Katrina. She was a sales assistant in a large haberdashers. She started spending the night with me.

When she slept with me, Katrina used to get up in the morning at six-thirty. The suburb where I lodged was a long way from the centre of the city where she worked. I will describe one of our mornings – but it could serve as a description of any of them:

I felt Katrina sliding out of bed. Behind the curtains the day glimmered palely. I told myself that I should get up but I seemed to lack the will to do so. I lay in bed as if paralysed and listened to Katrina getting ready.

Drying her face on a towel, Katrina came over to me. 'August, you must get up. It's time to get up,' she whispered shaking me gently. 'In a moment. Just give me another five minutes,' I replied sleepily and rolled over in the bed. Outside in the street I could hear the first workers making their way to work, clumping along the pavement and across cobbled streets in their clogs, while shouting coarsely to one another about their exploits the night before. The sensation of the world stirring and getting itself to work, while I lay stricken and unable to move, was peculiarly painful. If I had got up, as I knew only too well, I would have immediately felt better. But I was caught in a web like a figure in a fairytale.

Katrina came over fully dressed and smelling of scent, and sat down on the edge of the bed. I closed my eyes tightly and pretended to be deeply asleep. 'Goodbye August,' she said and kissed me on the forehead. 'I did try to wake you but you seemed so dead tired I thought it was best just to leave you.' (She said this every morning or a variation of it. What she meant was that she hadn't tried too hard to wake me. Only when I was asleep did she feel absolutely safe and certain that I was not going to leave her.)

'What time is it?' I murmured, stretching luxuriously under the covers and enjoying the sensation of the cold sheets on my legs. Then I added, 'Come back to bed?' 'Oh if only I could, my darling,' she replied, 'but it's nearly seven. I've got to go to work and you should be getting up yourself.' She kissed me again, on the mouth this time. Her lips were very full and soft. I can still feel the impression they made against my mouth (not to mention the way they ranged over the other parts of my body). 'Bye-bye,' I murmured. Then she asked me, in her quick nervous way, if I loved her and if she could meet me that evening. 'Yes yes,' I replied and nodded my head. I was always slightly irritated by these questions. Of course I loved her. I wouldn't have been seeing her if I hadn't. 'I love you too,' she said and kissed me again. 'You're going to be late,' I told her. 'Yes,' she said. She ruffled my hair, reluctantly got to her feet and slipped out the door.

As soon as the latch clicked shut and I could hear her clattering down the stone stairs towards our yard, I sprang out of bed. This was what happened every morning. It was as if the sound were a magic wand. One wave of it and my lethargy disappeared. I ran to the tap and splashed my face. The water was so cold it made my cheekbones ache. I threw open the window and called down to Katrina as she crossed the yard. 'Don't do anything I wouldn't do,' I shouted. 'See you tonight.' She waved back and mouthed something tender, then disappeared down the alleyway.

1981:
Afternoon

I came out of my office at a quarter to one. I was half an hour from Harold's lunch and dreading it.

In accounts Doris and Maureen were working away. Dennis, the other junior, was at his desk, holding a pen in his fat hand and laboriously copying something out. Emma was photocopying collecting sheets as they came out and collating them. In my younger days the sight of my employees working away had always filled me with a certain amount of pleasure, and I had taken pride in their industry. But those times were gone.

'I'm going now,' I said to Emma.' I'll see you and the others later.'

'Goodbye, August.' She put on her broadest smile, showing off a row of dazzling white teeth. The first year she worked for me she had saved up all her money to have them crowned and capped. When it was done she had said to me, 'Now that I can smile, at last I can find a husband.' It was shortly after that that she met Brad.

'See you later, alligator,' she called after me.

'In a while, crocodile,' I replied from the door.

I took a few gentle steps along the street and reminded myself of the resolution I had made that morning. Physical fitness was a prerequisite if I was going to break out of the shell. I began to hurry away.

On Your Marks, the local sportswear shop, smelt of carpet and pine. It was filled with brown-skinned mannequins in ski-wear and racks of air rifles. An assistant found me the most conventionally styled swimming trunks that were available and advised me which goggles to buy. As I waited for my cheque card to be

49

returned, an American came in with a portable video camera and asked how to get to Marble Arch. I listened to the assistant giving instructions as if I were hearing something happening a long way off. I came out of the shop with my plastic bag of goods and glanced at my watch. One o'clock. If I dragged my feet I would not get to the lunch until one ten. Fifty minutes and then I could decently leave. That was not a long time, I told myself.

Crowds flowed round me as I started to walk. I passed Ivy's the greengrocer's, and inhaled a smell of fruit, thick at the back of the throat. Portraits of Prince Charles and Lady Diana stared down at me from behind the window with red, white and blue tinsel hanging in loops above.

In the next shop a single silk dress hung in the window, which was otherwise empty except for a recent *Vogue* cover. Behind the door a girl in a sailor's suit was sticking a small hand-written sign to the glass: 'We shall be closed for the Royal Wedding.' My office would be shut too. Anticipation was beginning to grip the city. I could feel it in the air.

I tapped my chest. Of course it would be back to work on Thursday, I thought, but Harold would not be there. He was being given the end of the week off. It was David's first and last act of generosity to the luckless young man. After the farewell lunch I would never have to see Harold again.

A West Indian with paint flecks in his hair was standing outside Riley's, the betting shop.

'. . . and running down the inside with two furlongs to go . . .' came the radio commentator from inside.

Through the open doorway I glimpsed men alone at the the tables where chits were filled, offering their silent prayers.

'. . . and it's Lucky Fred first past the post. Lucky Fred followed by. . . .'

A man in overalls came out and kicked something into the air. Gambling always made me feel uneasy and the angry despair of failure most uncomfortable of all.

I turned the corner and saw the Coach and Horses looming ahead. Two figures were sitting on the bench outside. I instantly recognised Joe from his red Victorian army jerkin, and from the sandwich boards advertising a local antique market which were leaning against the pub wall behind him. Joe was a familiar figure in the area, parading with the boards in the morning and invariably drunk in the afternoon. At Christmas he used to come to the office with a Santa Claus tin and collect change. But the other man, tall, thin, gangling and wearing a double-breasted suit, the other man was a stranger.

'Hello, sir. Hello there,' said Joe, rising to his feet. 'Present and correct?' he added. He raised his hand to his battered velvet Beefeater's hat in a mock salute.

His face was covered with scabs like masticated red liquorice. When delirious from alcohol, Joe would shiver in doorways and scratch them until his skin bled. I had seen this myself.

'Will I be seeing you later, sir?' Joe asked. 'Will I have that pleasure? It's the Royal Wedding.'

Suddenly I became aware that the other man was staring at me.

'Yes, I'm sure you will,' I said.

I pressed the wood and stepped into the pub. The door shut automatically. I stared down the length of the room. A man in a suit was scraping a jar of salad dressing with a knife. Two women sat at the bar with their legs crossed, sipping gin and tonics as they slipped their shoes on and off. Harold was in the corner with a half-drunk pint.

It was a good opportunity to straighten matters out. From the adjacent public bar came the soft thud of darts and low cheers.

'Hello,' I said. 'You're early.'

The younger man lifted his head.

'Hello, Mr Slemic.'

'Please. August.'

Harold nodded. He was prepared to acknowledge the Christian name but that did not mean he would use it.

'Everything go all right with the Sikhs?' I asked.

'As well as could be expected under the circumstances,' Harold replied. 'They want to open a Sikh restaurant. I don't think they'll get permission.'

'Are they refugees?'

'I didn't ask.'

'Have you noticed something? After every political

51

upheaval, refugees always come to the West and open restaurants.'

'That's the West for you,' said Harold. 'We only register changes with our stomach. Let's hope nothing happens to Britain or we'll end up poisoning the world with fish and chips.'

'Yes,' I agreed, and laughed. 'I'm sorry about what happened,' I added.

'It can't be helped,' responded the younger man. 'It's just one of those things.' Apart from his mouth his face remained utterly still as he spoke.

'At least we shall be having a drink,' I said. 'Things would have come to a pretty sorry pass if we couldn't even do that.'

I put my swimming things on the chair and discovered what Harold was having. Then I went over to the bar and stared absentmindedly at the price list. Like the rest of the pub interior it was decked with more red, white and blue tinsel, and carried extra information about reduced prices and increased opening hours the following day. I moved a sodden beer mat and leaned on my elbow. The barman with his back to me was listening to a woman with ringed fingers.

'An entire lager went on my tits,' she said in a hoarse voice. 'I was fucking furious. And Miss La-di-da swanning about in her silk suspenders.'

The woman glanced theatrically in my direction and raised her eyes. She had black frizzy hair. The barman turned.

'Yes,' he said.

Carrying the glasses carefully I moved back to our table. Harold pushed out a chair for me and I sat down. We took our first sips of lager in silence.

'Listen,' I said finally, 'it had nothing to do with me. Do you understand?' I added.

'Sure.'

Harold performed one of his famous shrugs and looked around.

'Sure I do.'

52

I saw that Harold was smiling. I turned in my seat and looked towards the door. It was David with his briefcase which he was never without, Emma in a straw hat, Maureen, red-faced and breathless, Doris shining with her immaculate make-up, and Dennis with an *Evening Standard* in his pocket like a baton. I turned back to the table and revolved the wet glass on my beer mat. I had missed my chance, if I had ever had one.

'Hail fellow, well met,' I heard my partner booming to Harold down the length of the room.

Hypocrite, I thought. Hypocrite.

In the delicate tubes in the middle of my chest. I could feel the tremblings of heartburn starting up again.

The pub door opened and out of the corner of my eye I registered the figure of the tall gangling man who had stared at me outside the pub. He was hovering on the threshold. Joe was behind in the street. His Beefeater hat was sitting on his head at a ridiculous angle.

'Don't be a fucking idiot, Robbie,' slurred Joe.

Robbie, as the tall one was called, lurched forward. Joe grasped his friend's arm attempting to stop him, only to be shaken free. Joe waved his hand gesturing disgust and resignation to Robbie's fate. Robbie stepped forward and in. The door swung shut behind him. Robbie stood on the mat by the one-armed bandit. His arms hung by his sides like cudgels. He looked like a man who had stopped to think and then forgotten what he had been thinking about. I sensed Robbie glaring towards me and turned away.

'I'll get some refills,' I said.

'Your shout, is it?' said Dennis. Dennis did the same job as Harold and I had decided over lunch that he was probably not a bit sorry to see his colleague go. Dennis wore a blue suit with rounded lapels and a knitted woollen tie with yellow stripes. His hair was sandy and his eyes small and dark.

'My shout?' I queried.

'It means you're calling, so to speak,' said Dennis. With

his short stocky frame and his thick thighs, Dennis had earned the nickname 'The Troll' in the office.

'Oh be quiet,' chimed Doris, her beauty spot moving as she spoke. 'If I got a pound every time you opened your mouth, Dennis, I could retire.'

'What are you having, Doris?' I asked.

'You're a gentleman, Mr Slemic. Dubonnet and lemon with extra ice, thank you.'

'I'll have a pint of Guinness, guv,' said Dennis, draining his glass and handing it to me. Emma asked for a white wine and Perrier water, and Maureen, for a Bacardi and slimline Coke. She was on a diet, she said.

'Anyone know what Harold and David are drinking?' I enquired.

Emma turned in her seat. David and Harold were standing together at the bar, feet jauntily resting on the brass footrail underneath. David had his arm across Harold's shoulder, half-covering up the 'All Stars' signature on the back of his famous baseball jacket. The two men were talking to the woman with the rings on her fingers and they were laughing.

'I think they've got some drinks,' said Emma.

As she turned back towards the table something caught Emma's eye. She made a face and glanced down at the carpet.

I caught her expression. I casually reached for my wallet and glanced towards the ground. On the carpet beside me there were two Hush Puppy shoes with sockless legs sticking out of them. There was also a whiff of urine. It was Robbie.

What could he possibly want?

I pulled out my wallet and started to tap it on my hand.

Robbie was standing right in the way of my path to the bar. If I got up, I would have to push him aside. I could feel, or I thought I could feel, Robbie's blue and enraged eyes scorching the back of my head. My knees began to waver.

'What's your problem, pal?' asked Dennis, looking up at Robbie.

Robbie stuck his right hand in front of my chin.

'Money,' he whispered.

In the background I heard the door opening.

'Come back here, you daft cunt,' called Joe from the street.

'I'm going to get the publican,' said Dennis.

'It's all right,' I said.

The wavering that had started in my knees had spread all the way down my calves. My mind was a complete blank.

'What were the orders again?' I asked.

As everyone called out, I opened my wallet, found something crinkly and passed it back over my shoulder deliberately without looking at it. The bank note was snatched from my hand.

'You dirty old tramp! That's far too much for you,' shouted Dennis. He stood up and wrenched it back.

Robbie's mouth dropped open. He raised his arms to try and grab the note but let them drop again.

'Oi,' it was the barman leaning across the bar, wagging his finger at Robbie. His face was square with fishy eyes. 'Get out,' he ordered.

'I want my money back. It's rightfully mine,' said Robbie, in a broad Scottish accent.

'Ten pounds is too much for you,' said Dennis. 'You'll only drink it. Now you heard the man.' He pointed towards the barman. 'Get out.'

I had to rectify the situation and knew what I had to do. I pulled fifty pence from my pocket and stood up.

'Here we are.'

I put the coin onto Robbie's long, spade-like palm which was criss-crossed with faint lines.

'I think you had better go,' I said, 'before the barman throws you out.'

Robbie bunched his hand into a fist and briefly saluted his gratitude.

'Hey! What do you say?' said Dennis. 'Come on.'

'Th . . . thanks,' stuttered Robbie.

He turned on his heels and began to speed towards the door. The seam of his jacket was torn and his trousers flapped around his bare ankles.

'Pathetic, isn't it? Makes you want to weep,' said Dennis.

'If I see you in here again,' the barman shouted, 'I'll set Rosie on you.'

The frizzy haired woman laughed. 'Yeah. I'll teach him,' she cackled. Harold and David laughed with her.

The pub door opened and shut.

Dennis offered me my ten-pound note back.

'It could have been a very expensive lunch.'

'Thank you,' I said.

'It's a very easy mistake to make,' said Emma. 'I'm sure I'm always giving more than I mean to when I'm asked for money in the street. You get nervous.'

'That was very well done Dennis,' said Doris. 'You showed great presence of mind.'

'Yes, I'm very grateful to you, Dennis,' I said.

'Fame at last,' cried Dennis, sitting back in his seat. 'Praise from the boss. More, more. . . .'

Doris scraped some uneaten steak and kidney pie onto a plate with a plastic knife.

'We'd better get this lot cleared if we're going to do some serious drinking,' she said. 'And that means you as well, Dennis. Just because you're a hero, it doesn't mean you're excused.'

Dennis took some paper napkins and folded them into triangles. Maureen screwed the top on to the mustard jar. I went over to the bar and ordered the drinks.

'Sorry about that, sir,' apologised the barman.

'It was nothing.'

'No matter what you do, you just can't keep them out. You know what I found those two doing the other day? Eating the geraniums in the pot outside. Honestly I did, Rosie. I told them geraniums were poisonous. That stopped them, the little bastards. Of course they're quite harmless really. That one who wears the uniform, he used to be a professor. Did you know that? Then he fell in love. The usual story. Sometimes at night I get him to show me all the stars. He knows all the Latin names. And that Scottish one. You ought to hear him sing. I'm sure he used to be a tenor. Beautiful voice. He can do *Auld Lang Syne* and bring tears to your eyes.'

I returned with the drinks. While the others talked I sat drinking mine in silence. I was aware of Emma looking at me half a dozen times but I did not return her gaze. I still felt a little foolish about the ten-pound note, and I didn't mind her thinking I was sulking.

'Have you heard Harold's good news?'

I looked around and saw David coming towards me. He was picking the silver foil off a champagne bottle.

'No,' I said.

Harold set a tray down at the other end of the table with seven long-stemmed glasses on it.

'Oohh, champagne. My favourite,' said Doris.

'It's not champagne, Doris. It's Veuve du Vernay. It's a sparkling wine made like champagne. It's called méthode champenoise.'

It was Dennis speaking, Dennis who regarded himself, I knew, as something of a wine expert. In his wallet I had seen a vintage guide and sometimes he used to return from lunch with bottles which he claimed were bargains.

Doris opened a powder compact, looked into the tiny mirror and began to fluff up her hair. Maureen wriggled in her seat. 'We always have champagne at Christmas,' she said.

'And what is the good news?' I asked.

'Harold's got a cracker of a job,' said David. 'Guaranteed, providing we give him a good reference. And his old lady's going to have one. . . .'

David poked me in the stomach and flopped down in his chair.

'Yes, it's a great day all round,' he shouted.

He pulled off the silver foil, rolled it into a pellet and dropped it into the ashtray.

'. . . and we're going to give him a reference, aren't we? We're going to give him the best bloody reference that can be got.'

David unscrewed the wire fastener around the top of the bottle and pulled it away.

'Yes, of course,' I said. 'That's excellent news.'

'You heard him, Harold,' David shouted enthusiastically. From the other end of the table Harold looked at me across the glasses and the beer mats.

'Yes, I heard him,' Harold said and smiled weakly.

The others mumured their congratulations.

David squeezed the cork and slowly began to twist.

'Don't move the cork, move the bottle,' advised Dennis. ''That way the energy is directed back, not forwards.'

'Lucky we drink so much bubbly at home,' David said,

ignoring Dennis, 'otherwise I wouldn't know how to open it. . . .'

'Why didn't you tell me your news before, Harold?' I asked.

It seemed more than odd that Harold had not come to me for the reference when David was clearly the enemy.

'I didn't have the opportunity to tell you,' replied Harold. 'Did I?'

'He was saving it for me,' interrupted David. He turned towards Harold. 'Now don't you worry, my son. You're going to get that reference. I've promised. He's promised.'

He pointed his thumb towards me.

'You're going to get that job and we're going to have you in competition with Slemic and Co. if it's the last thing I do before the wife kills me. . . .'

David made a face and winked dramatically.

The cork screeched as he twisted the bottle.

'All right, everybody,' Dennis called. 'Mind your eyes. These things can be very dangerous.'

There was a dull pop as the cork came away from the glass stem.

David leaned forward and poured the pale-coloured liquid into the first glass. It bubbled up and white froth spilt over the side.

'Don't waste it. Steady on . . .' someone called.

'Bring in the greyhounds. They can lap it up,' said Maureen laughing.

The glasses were full.

'Ladies and gentlemen,' boomed David, 'a toast. . . . To Harold and his future, and may he have every possible success. Not forgetting the baby of course. . . .'

'Speech, speech,' called everyone.

Harold rose slowly to his feet.

'Unaccustomed as I am to speaking in public. . . .'

There were titters of laughter.

'As I am accustomed to speaking in public.'

'Get on with it,' called Dennis.

'. . . I shall keep this short and sweet. Nor shall I tell any rude jokes.'

'Oh go on, do,' said Maureen.

'. . . well, maybe later. I've had a wonderful time at Slemic and Co. and I shall always remember it fondly.

58

I'm a bit disappointed I haven't been given a gold watch – I won't make any bones about it – but I will be bringing away with me something much more important. Happy memories. And that's the most important thing you can bring away with you from anywhere. Slemic and Co. are a small firm, but they've managed to hold on to something very important which is all too often forgotten in this day and age. They still offer a personal service. So ladies and gentlemen, I offer a toast. To Mr Slemic. And long may he offer a personal service.'

'To Mr Slemic,' everyone chorused.

Now it was my turn to stand. I didn't need to be encouraged. Stutterers can go on stage and act as if they have no impediment, and I'm the same when it comes to speaking in public. My reticence evaporates, and I find as I stand up that I know instantly what I have to say and how I am going to say it.

'Today is a sad day,' I began. 'It's always a sad day when someone with whom you've worked leaves the company. But it's also a happy day too because Harold is going on to better and brighter things. You can't stand still. Life is full of change. If it didn't, it wouldn't be life, would it?'

'He's getting philosophical,' said Dennis.

'I've seen many changes in my own life, in Poland where I come from, and here in England, the country which has been so good to me. Some for the better, and some for the worse. In life, when everything is boiling up, especially when things look as though they're going to get worse, one always wishes that everything could stand still. At least I always do. But after the event, be it good, bad, or indifferent, isn't one always happy the way things have turned out? We know good and bad, we laugh and we cry, but the world is slowly becoming a better place, isn't it? And even something small, like Harold's leaving us, is part of that gradual change for the better. So ladies and gentlemen, I give you a toast. To Harold and to a better future. . . .'

'You know, you should have been a poet,' said David and everyone agreed.

* * *

59

At school in my Classics class, I had learnt that in the middle of the body there was an empty space between the organs called the hypochondrium. Here, I imagined, pain collected like water in a barrel. When it was full the pain trickled out and began its wandering odyssey, causing the aches and pains which could not be pinned down.

At four-thirty I stood up from my desk. I was sore somewhere in my pelvis. I put my hands on my hips and arched backwards. For a moment I imagined I looked like a cheap line-drawn advertisement for slipped disc sufferers, of the kind I used to stare at in the Sunday newspapers amongst the garden sheds, Guernsey smocks and ladies' glamourwear catalogues. The action brought no relief.

What had I done that day? Of all the events, it was the Coach and Horses that stuck out most clearly. The pub had been dark and damp, smelling of beer slops, and in the gloom Robbie's eyes had shone bright and piercing. With his tall thin body Robbie had been a serpent, moving on his coils with his head upright. I had attracted the serpent's antagonism because of my cowardice. This thought made me uneasy. Where did these strange fantasies come from? When they were particularly wild I even wondered if I was losing my reason. But just as they came, these little odd periods, so they also went, and the normal everyday sensations returned, a layer of snow overlaying bare earth.

Now the clock was creeping towards five, I remembered why I had got up. I was going to get the files and the keys and Emma and I were going to re-address them.

I opened my door and looked along the outside office. Emma was at her desk. Round the corner, hidden out of sight, the door of the accounts office stood open. 'I've re-wallpapered the lounge,' I heard Maureen saying. 'I think you'll like it. It's got little red flowers all over it. And there's a new settee.'

I walked forward and glanced in her direction. Maureen was alone, speaking on the telephone. From the way she was curled over the receiver I could have guessed that the conversation was private if I had not already overheard.

Maureen and her husband had come south from Scotland when her husband had been made manager of a supermarket in Catford, and she had been working in Slemic and Co. for over five years. She was a plump and lively woman, and on St Valentine's Day a jumbo sized envelope always arrived for her. When she failed to display it but put it away in the drawer of her desk, rumours naturally started circulating concerning her private life.

I opened the cupboard door and began to pile the keys into a box which had once held a ream of paper. I had taken it from under the photocopying machine where we kept such things.

'Well, where do you think the money for the re-decorating came from?' Maureen's voice drifted through the open door.

I turned my head to listen.

'Jamie's been slaving at Tesco's,' she continued.

Now whoever was on the other end of the line was speaking. I placed the keys more silently.

'You needn't worry about that. He's in the Lake District,' Maureen said reassuringly.

'. . . No. Walking . . . Of course I live in Lewisham. . . . Don't be like that, Tony. I said Dulwich because you go through Dulwich to get to Lewisham. . . . You just get yourself to Vauxhall Bridge and follow my map. I'll put it in the post tonight.'

I felt I had done wrong. What right had I to eavesdrop on another? To probe into their life without their knowing? To have any authority in an office one had to be above all that.

I closed the cupboard door loudly and marched into the accounts office. I wanted to be certain that my presence was announced. Maureen looked up from the telephone and blushed.

'Just a second,' she almost whispered into the mouthpiece. 'It's my boss.'

She stared up at me with a guilty look. She had a round, puffy face of the sort it was almost impossible to picture in the imagination. She wore blue eye-shadow and orange lipstick on her little mouth.

'Sorry to disturb you,' I said pleasantly. 'It's nearly five. Why don't you go home early?'

61

'That's very kind of you.'

She smiled, her blue eyes twinkled and she was suddenly attractive.

'Where's Doris?' I asked.

I glanced down at her desk. Several photostated pages from the south-east London section of the A-Z lay there sellotaped together. From one corner to the other a thick red line zig-zagged across. So this was how her visitor was to navigate his way to her door. There was something tender, innocent and painfully hopeful about it.

'She's gone down to the DHSS,' said Maureen.

'Well if you do see her, tell her to go home.'

'Yes, I will, and thank you.'

I turned round and walked with my box of keys back to the door.

'I'm so looking forward to seeing you, my dear,' I heard Maureen saying when I was just outside. 'So, so much. I. . . .'

Her voice was filled with yearning. But what if her lover did not turn up? I could just see Maureen on the new settee, her eyes filled with tears and little balls of wet tissue strewn around her. I wanted her to be happy. I wanted Emma to be happy. I felt a great rush of benevolence towards everyone hurrying by in the street.

'Well Emma,' I said with a broad smile. 'Any old iron?'

I jigged the box up and down, tumbling the keys inside.

'Shall we commence battle then?' she said, smiling, 'and sort out this little mess?'

I closed the door and we sat down in my office. I held the keys and called out the numbers. She went through the lists until she found the corresponding figures. She had a round face and thin arching eyebrows like my mother's. Her fingers were short and the nails filed into smooth curves. She wore two wedding rings. A plain gold band and an engagement ring with a stone. From time to time she looked up and smiled back at me tentatively.

When we had finished she said, 'Cup of tea?'

'No. Let's have a drink,' I said.

She widened her eyes with mock horror. 'I had too much at lunchtime and now you're encouraging me again.'

'Go on. You don't have to work tomorrow.'

'All right, then. Just a little one.'

I returned from the drinks cabinet with a tray holding a large glass of Dubonnet for her and a sherry for myself.

'Your health,' I said, settling myself in my seat and holding up my glass.

'God, this is enormous. Cheers,' she replied.

She drank back half the glass.

'I shall be drunk,' she said. 'I hope I don't say anything indiscreet.'

'How are you?' I asked.

'How am I?'

'Mmm. . . .'

She swallowed another mouthful.

'I'm all right. I'm fairly all right.'

'Only fairly all right?' I asked.

'Am I feeling drunk already?'

I raised my arms and shrugged my shoulders.

'How are things at home?' I asked.

'They're not ideal,' she began. 'My husband – I know I can trust you – he still likes a flutter now and again.'

'He likes to gamble. Yes, you told me that already,' I said.

'So I did. I'd forgotten. I must be drunk.'

Her glass was already empty. I fetched the Dubonnet bottle, refilled it and put it on the desk in front of her.

'He's a gambler,' she continued. 'He'll leave it alone for months and then he'll suddenly get the urge. I can see it coming. He begins to get shifty and nervous and to stay out late. Then he disappears and I know he's on a binge. He doesn't come home for three days, four days, a week, not until he's spent everything. Then he's always sorry and I lose my top and then we always make up.'

She drank from her re-filled glass, draining it by half.

'Has he been doing it recently?' I asked.

'No, not recently. Not since just before Christmas. But I can see it coming on again. I know him so well. I can just tell.'

We talked on, Emma becoming affected by the drink. When I suggested that she and her husband might receive some help from an organisation which existed to help gamblers and their families, she brushed it aside. She was not interested in solving the problem, only interested in talking about it to an older man whom she could trust. I felt disappointed. As her feelings towards me were clearly those of a daughter, it therefore followed that the only feelings which I would be permitted would be those of a father.

'I must tell you the funniest thing,' Emma said.

She was on her fourth Dubonnet.

'Once he came back from a spree without spending all his money. I said I'd take him back if he promised not to gamble any more. He said he wouldn't. Life went back to normal. We got on very well. We always do after he's been on the rampage. Then one evening he didn't show up. Just like that. No warning. I was absolutely furious. I'd cooked this big dinner as a surprise. I'd been looking forward to a really nice evening in. The next morning he came home all dark and moody. I said, "Where have you been?" He wouldn't tell me, but I knew damn well. I said, "You've been gambling. You've been in some club." And he said, "All right. I had some money left over. I went to the Edgware Road and I lost it all." Now it's not as if he hadn't gambled before. But I'd somehow thought things were going to be different because he hadn't spent all the money. I went absolutely mad. I got the dinner out of the 'fridge and started throwing it on the table in front of him. I said, "I was bloody waiting for you last night having cooked this and you were bloody frittering away our money." Then I started picking the roast chicken I'd cooked to bits and trying to push pieces of it into his mouth. He went berserk. He started pushing me about. "Don't you get uppity with me, lady," he said, and all of that. I tried to get out the door but he got there before me. "You touch me and I'll have the police on to you," I shouted. I was livid too. He threw me onto the ground and got on top of me. It was just like being back in the school playground. "I'm going to teach you a lesson," he said. He got the chicken and started trying to make me eat it. "Go on," he said. "You spent so much time making this, why don't you have some?" I spat it out. He tried it again. As I lay there I thought, "I hate this," and then I realised, "No, I'm enjoying it. I can be the baby for a change." '

Emma looked at me and smiled at me and I smiled back.

'I really must be drunk,' she said. 'I've never told anyone that before.'

I liked being the boss to whom she told her secrets. But to have a life presented to me with unhappy patterns which mirrored my own – no.

'I think I might make a move,' I said. 'I'm going to stop at the baths on the way home. Why don't you call it a day too?'

'That's very kind of you,' she said. 'but I've got something I'd like to finish if I can still type. And I'm meeting my husband later in town – we're going to the Royal Fireworks. So I have to stay.'

She sprang up.

'I'll wash your glass for you.'

It was as if the conversation had not happened.

She smiled and left the room clinking the two glasses. I put the Dubonnet bottle back in the cabinet. I had been wrong to expect anything from the conversation. I collected my carrier bag and went outside.

The swimming baths were a red brick municipal building, surrounded by low blocks of flats and cherry trees. It was also the public laundry and mistakenly I entered the launderette where a tired woman with a shopping basket full of sheets re-directed me. I bought my ticket in a splendid marble hall, spoilt by notice boards advertising aerobics classes and a soft drink dispenser, and undressed on sticky tiles surrounded by shouting boys.

The pool was enormous with a curved glass roof supported by metal beams. Walking along the edge I felt self-conscious of my stomach and pulled it in. The swimming pool smell was powerful and heady. I moistened my goggles as I had been told to, placed them over my eyes and climbed into the shallow end. The water was cold as I started to swim, but within two or three strokes I had adjusted to the temperature. I lifted my head out of the water to look at the clock hanging over the deep end and gave myself a target. So many lengths in so many minutes.

I had started the new regime. This was the first step along the long road that would lead to my floating on the surface with legs outstretched, ready at any moment to fly away on my gorgeous dragonfly wings.

I moved quite fast through the water, overtaking two young girls in bathing hats who were talking to one another as they performed a leisurely back-stroke. Perhaps I was not so unhealthy after all? The coldness of the water and the exercise added to my sense of well-being. Every day there were trials and torments. They always seemed large at the time but in retrospect they shrank to their real size. I felt the rain-clouds were clearing and sunshine was coming.

At the start of my fifteenth length I pushed off from the shallow end more slowly. The inside of my nose was tingling from the chlorine and the skin on the ends of my fingers felt crinkled. Where the water became deeper I switched from the breast-stroke to the crawl. The tiles below were a blue shimmer. I saw two children who had dropped to the bottom rising upwards like pearl fishermen from an ocean bed. My ears were filled now with water, now with shrieks and cries. But above the hubbub I could hear one voice shouting. I grasped the lip running across the deep end and lifted my head.

'I saw you. . . .' I heard the voice calling loudly.

I turned and saw, floating by the wooden steps, a man with straggly hair and a pair of spectacles incongruously perched on the end of his nose. He was waving his finger at a huddle of boys.

'I saw what you did . . .' the man continued hoarsely.

The boys were all thin and shivering, their arms held across their chests for warmth, and with barely restrained smirks on their faces. Suddenly they took hold of one of their group and pushed him screeching towards the edge.

'One, two, three, whey. . . .'

The thin, white body of the victim tumbled into the water lop sidely and the man was splashed all over his face and spectacles.

'How dare you,' the man shouted. 'I'll box your ears.'

The boys started laughing as the man waved his fist. He was like an enormous animal floating in the water.

Just as I was wondering whether I should swim over I noticed a lifeguard slowly padding towards the huddle. He was a well-tanned young man with a whistle around his neck. I found the wall with my feet and pushed off. Five more lengths and I would be on target.

When I was finished I climbed out of the water and found my towel on the silver radiator where I had left it. I rubbed my back vigorously. The material was coarse on my skin. Then I showered, exchanged my rubber wristband for my basket of clothes and selected a corner in which to change. Pulling on my trousers, I noticed my body was pleasantly aching and beads of perspiration had sprung up on my forehead. I sat down on the bench and rolled up my trouser bottoms. At the other end of the changing room I noticed the man with spectacles – the madman, as I had come to think of him. He was heading towards the counter. The man's body was fat and white, but his puffy ankles were a deep purple colour, like lilac.

I dried between my toes and pulled a sock from my shoe. The white bulk was bearing towards me just as I had expected. I looked up. A pair of paisley underpants dangled from one of the cross bars in the man's basket, and on top of the clothes piled in the bottom rested a sailor's hat with a white peak. It was the sort of headgear which I connected with middle-aged men who messed about with boats at weekends.

'You've got to be carefuul of the young children,' the man said, banging his basket down, 'particularly the young girls.'

I recognised the man's accent as Irish.

'They're very dangerous.' The Irishman's thin hair was standing upright and he looked comical. 'They had the "monster" in this afternoon. You know, the big floating thing with all the kids playing on it?'

I nodded. I remembered the large floating contraption made of rubber, which I had passed every length I did.

'The thing is,' the Irishman continued confidentially, 'they jump off it, you know. That's the thing. And if you're not careful, you end up touching their breasts. I had to have words with them about it.'

I pulled on my second sock and looked across. The Irishman's face was wide and flat, with a small nose and deep creases. There was something unborn about it.

I slipped my feet into my shoes and began to tie my laces. The Irishman turned and modestly began to lower his trunks. When they were around his knees they dropped to the ground and he stepped out of them. I was amazed to see that his buttocks were even whiter than the rest of his body. He picked up the towel from the bench and turned to wrap it around his middle. For a fraction of a second his groin was uncovered and I saw that his penis and testicles were the same size as those of a pre-pubescent boy. They were tiny, white as a shell, smooth and hairless.

The Irishman flopped down on the bench. His glasses had slipped and he pushed them up his nose.

'You know what?' he said.

'What?' I said.

'I was the heaviest baby born this century. I was thirteen pounds. Only my mother died two years ago, so she couldn't verify.'

'Where were you born?' I asked.

'In Ireland.'

'I know you were born in Ireland. I meant whereabouts in Ireland?'

'Ennis.'

'In County Clare?'

'You know it?' The Irishman dusted water off his small, red nipples.

'I had my honeymoon there in the Old Grounds Hotel.' I remembered the ivy-covered building as I spoke.

'Know anyone in it who knows me?' asked the Irishman pugnaciously.

'I wouldn't think so,' I said, 'I had my honeymoon a long time ago. Nineteen fifty-four.'

'I've been out of it over forty-five years, mind you. Came over here in nineteen thirty-four. Two days later I joined up. Yes sir, the Irish Guards.'

He stretched his paisley underpants and clumsily put one purple foot and then the other through their holes.

'What happened in the war?' I enquired.

'I was in the war but I was never in the firing line. They kept me back on account of poor eyesight.'

The underpants were on and the towel came away. The paisley briefs stretched around the enormous middle seemed ridiculous.

'Are you a military man yourself?'

'No,' I lied. Mention the RAF, I thought, and it would lead to an interminable exchange.

The Irishman began to button himself into a yellow, drip-dry shirt. The conversation turned to the topic of his relatives, all of whom were in senior positions in the English or Irish police.

I wrung my trunks into the channel along the middle of the floor.

'I must go. Goodbye,' I said firmly. Family connections amongst the police had begun to test my patience.

I made my way past the young boys who had tormented the Irishman – they were flicking one another with wet towels – and handed my basket across the counter. A black attendant with cropped hair took it from me sulkily.

In the passage outside I stopped in front of the hair-dryer and dropped ten pence in the slot. I took the metal tube and pointed it at my head. I felt hot air on my scalp and down my neck. I closed my eyes and basked in the warm flow. The conversation with the Irish Guardsman had stirred long forgotten memories: bumping through the streets of Ennis in a taxi holding hands with Eunice, bicycles with the old carbide lamps drifting past the car windows, the hotel in the evening light, the ivy-covered walls rustling in the wind. . . .

'Have you finished, mister?' The dryer clicked and the soporific flow of air came to an abrupt stop. I opened my eyes. A girl with wet hair and a remarkably white face stood behind me. Her eyes red from chlorine were already rimmed with black mascara. She was wearing a white leather skirt and white boots. 'Yes, I have, I have,' I said, touching my forehead.

Something had been there, within my grasp, and now it was gone.

In the corner there was a table. I went over and tipped everything out of my wallet. From the dryer the girl looked at me and I paid no attention. I rummaged through the pile in front of me: bank notes, a Mass card in Polish, my AA membership, stubs for the dry cleaner's, old books of postage stamps and receipts – until at last I found the square of newsprint which I was looking for. It was small and grubby and as fragile as tissue. I opened it out with extreme care until it was flat. 'Squirrel loves her Mongoose,' I read. It was a St Valentine's Day message placed in *The Times* by Eunice the year after we married. Squirrel had been Eunice's nickname in those days because of her habit of sleeping under the covers as if she were hibernating. When we were alone and I called her 'Squirrel' she would hold her hands up like paws and twitch her face. How we had laughed together over it. My own nickname had no specific origin. It was just what she had come up with one night and it had stuck.

'Squirrel loves her Mongoose.' I read it again and waited. I expected to feel a tremor of feeling, or something, nostalgia. I was not certain what. But I felt nothing.

I repacked my wallet and returned it to my breast pocket. It pressed against my chest like a growth. I began to walk down the corridor. Swimming-pool smells gave way to wax. My heels clicked on the tiles. A wide set of marble stairs lay at the end, with a gleaming brass rail running up the side. I walked back through the marble hall passing the ticket kiosk. Recent memories of the Irishman were mingling with faraway ones of my honeymoon and the early years of my marriage. The Irishman was a warning to me. If I did not live a full life, life, and even my generative powers, would literally desert me. Up to that moment I had imagined my future as being secured through transformation. I was hard and calcinated but I would lose my casing: I would become a beautiful creature with whirring wings and a body the colour of petrol. Now I saw the way ahead in much simpler and more direct terms. The world was rich: I just had to learn to grasp the opportunities that came my way. The new regime and its attempts at self-transformation were all very well but what mattered was a complete change of attitude. I had to stop thinking and I had to start acting.

I pushed through the brass swing doors. The bark of

the cherry trees in the street outside was plum-coloured, just like the cherry trees at my uncle Peter's.

I imagine Emma met her husband outside MacDonald's at Marble Arch. They bought root beers and dashed through the honking traffic to Hyde Park. It was already beginning to fill with crowds in anticipation of the Royal Wedding fireworks. They found a place on the grass under a tree.

'How was your day?' asked Brad. 'Anything nice happen?'

'I had a long talk with my boss,' said Emma. 'He's a nice man but he's not happy you know. It's a shame because he deserves to be.'

'You see too much of your boss, if you ask me,' said Brad.

'Are you jealous?'

'Yeah, I'm jealous,' said Brad, squeezing her above the knee until she shrieked with laughter and threatened to pour her drink on him.

December 29th 1980

Today is Monday, the first day back at work. There is nothing to do except write in my little notebook.

I stepped from the big room of our Warsaw flat onto the balcony. I was eleven years old. Bells were sounding across the city, calling worshippers to mass. I looked down. A woman in a wide-brimmed hat moved quickly along. The cobbles under her feet were gleaming in the sun.

On the corner I could see the old flower-seller standing by her stall. She was wearing her white turban which she wore only on Sunday. She had roses, carnations and chrysanthemums for sale and they stood in metal jugs. I had heard it whispered around the neighbourhood that she helped out girls when they were in trouble (although I had no idea what that meant). I was frightened by her, and whenever I had to pass her stall, I would always cross the street.

Someone was moving in our apartment. I went back inside. Through the door of the living room I could see my mother in the hall. I went past the piano running all my fingers over the keys and at a rush all the notes tumbled out, one after the other.

I emerged into the hall just in time to see my mother turning the corner at the end. I knew instantly where she was going. I ran down the side hallway after her and did not stop until I reached the door of my brother's bedroom.

I looked in. His room was square with a fireplace in

one corner and a bed in the other. The curtains were pulled tightly over the window. My brother lay propped up on white pillows. His face was round and white with bluish shadings under the eyes.

'How are you, darling?' mother whispered.

She sat on the edge of the bed and began to smooth back his hair. Matted by perspiration it had stuck to his forehead.

'I think I've got a temperature', my brother said, stressing each of the syllables.

His medicines were on the bedside table. They stood in big bottles to which were stuck labels covered with illegible handwriting. My mother tipped the thermometer from the silver sheath in which it lived and slipped it under his tongue.

'Close your mouth, darling.'

She took his wrist with her long fingers. Before she married she had been a nurse. Involuntarily I sought my own pulse, laying my fingers on my thin bones.

'Don't stand in the doorway, August,' she said quietly. 'Either come in or go out.'

I stepped forward. Was I feeling something in my wrist? I asked myself. My mother had once told me that when I could find my own pulse, I would stop being a boy and start becoming a man. I was impatient for this to happen. I screwed up my eyes and concentrated. There was definitely a fluttering feeling at the end of my fingertips but it wasn't the solid rhythm she had described to me.

I dropped my arms to my side and opened my eyes again. Across the room I saw that my mother was holding a small fob which she kept in her pocket and counting, her lips moving silently.

'Well, everything seems to be all right in that department,' she said returning the watch to her pocket.

'Do you have pain?' She stroked the back of his hand.

My brother nodded.

'In your head? Here and here?' She touched the spots over each temple.

He nodded again.

'And in your tummy?'

'Yes.'

She slipped the thermometer from his mouth and

74

started to twist it carefully. I thought I caught a glimpse of the mercury like a fish underwater.

'It's a hundred. That's not bad. You were a hundred and one yesterday.'

'Does that mean I'm getting better?' whispered my brother.

'You're on the mend. Yes.'

She wiped the end of the thermometer with cotton wool soaked in antiseptic and returned it to its case.

'August and your mama are probably going over to uncle Peter's. Will that be all right?'

Again my brother nodded, yes.

'You won't be lonely. Rita will be here. She'll look after you. A little bird told me she was going to read you the story of Sinbad the Sailor.'

'I think I'll just sleep. I feel very tired,' replied my brother.

He closed his eyes and turned his large, moon-shaped face to the side. His breathing became calm and easy.

'My poor darling,' she said.

She smoothed his forehead. My brother murmured something, sighed and appeared to fall asleep. Then my mother turned and put her finger to her lips. Misha was always falling asleep and she was forever, it seemed, motioning me to be silent. But it was never I who fell asleep so that others had to be quiet on account of me. I was not, it seemed, a child to whom adults were deferential, as they were to my brother. Her gesture that I be quiet was a reminder to me of this and I loathed it.

I slipped from the sick room and went out to the long freckled mirror that hung in the hallway. I was wearing the sailor's suit which I only wore on Sundays in the summer. The white cotton smelt of starch and Rita mixed together. I looked at my hair which was short and dark, my long pale face and my narrow shoulders. The fact that they were not widening out like my father's was a worry to me. I feared that I was not going to grow up to be a man like him, and my inability to find my pulse confirmed this. I puffed my chest out and at that moment my mother appeared at my side.

'Do I look nice?' she asked, her reflection showing in the mirror beside mine. She too had a long pale face and beautiful grey eyes. Her hair was pinned up and her silver earrings swayed from side to side. She was wearing her best dress. It was blue and gathered into a fan at the back.

'Oh yes,' I said.

'Very, very nice?'

'Oh yes,' I agreed.

'Now go and say goodbye to your father.'

I found my way along the passage at the back to his door. This was the quietest part of the apartment because it was furthest from the lift. I knocked on the dark wood, twice.

'Enter,' said a voice from within.

I opened the door. My father was sitting at his desk in front of the small window overlooking the courtyard. The yellow strongbox which he usually kept locked was open on the floor beside him.

'I've come to say goodbye,' I said.

I stopped behind his chair and looked down. The lock with its key stuck in it hung down from the hasp. I could see the box was filled with forms and documents and I remembered my mother telling me that locks of my baby hair and my milk teeth were kept there in an envelope.

'You shouldn't look at other people's private papers,' I heard my father saying.

I thought about telling him that I was looking for the envelope of teeth and hair but I doubted if he would have believed it.

His bearded lips pressed against my forehead.

'Don't get up to any mischief,' he said.

He turned back towards his desk. I glanced longingly once more at the box, turned and ran out of the room.

I caught the tram with my mother and we found seats side by side near the door. We set off with a jolt. The streets of the city boiled beyond the windows. A group of soldiers in their shirt sleeves, their jackets thrown over their shoulders stood nearby. I noticed the woman opposite. Her face was terrifically wide, with traces of perspiration on her temples under her dyed black hair. Between thick fingers with bitten nails she was holding a large, coloured fan which she wielded with enormous dexterity.

Hot and tired, we arrived at the distant suburb where

76

my uncle lived. Uncharacteristically my mother bought a bunch of flowers. She asked the flower-seller to wrap them and he presented them to me wrapped in white tissue paper.

'Perhaps the little gentleman would care to carry them,' he said.

We walked through suburban streets under shading rows of chestnut and elm. The sun lit up the leaves overhead and patterns of dark and shade played on the ground under our feet. The flowers dripped and some of the now sodden tissue paper fell away. In the villas on either side voices sounded and in one I heard a piano playing. It was a Sunday morning and everything was exactly as it always was except that I was without my brother. His absence was like a missing tooth in the mouth, into which the tongue cannot stop probing.

We reached my uncle's villa. I pulled on the metal stirrup. The bell tinkled far away inside the house. My mother pressed my hair down and rearranged the collar of my sailor suit.

'How handsome you look today,' she said.

The air smelt of her scent as she tipped the bottle onto her wrist and touched behind her ears. Her earrings swayed. First the Judas hole and then the door scraped back. Maya of the broad face stood before us soothing down her white starched apron. We walked across the paving stones of the front garden. The line of mock cherries stretched beside us. The bark was purplish – the colour of plums. The front door was open. My uncle came out in his check suit. He was sweating. He rubbed his face with his handkerchief.

'Welcome. You are a thousand times welcome,' he called. We climbed the stone steps worn in the middle. Childish cries attracted my attention. I looked over the wall at the side. In the next garden there were children playing Blind Man's Buff: an elder sister, bare-footed, was there with a white scarf around her head, her brothers around her, darting about like fish in shallow water.

My uncle's hand came towards me, the gold signet ring on the podgy little finger. We shook hands formally. His grasp was firm.

'How are you today?'

'Very well,' I replied.

I handed him the flowers. He thanked me.

'Where's your brother?' he asked.

'He's not very well,' my mother interrupted. 'We left him at home. You'll just have to make do with us today.'

'Please let August tell me,' responded my uncle. 'He's got a tongue in his head, hasn't he?'

My uncle leant towards me.

'Well?' he asked. 'Where is Misha?'

'Misha's not very well,' I stammered.

'I said, "Where is Misha?" ' continued my uncle.

I started to go red. 'Misha's at home,' I said.

'Thank you.'

My uncle turned to my mother and took her by the hand.

'The most beautiful woman in the world,' he said.

He brought her fingers to his lips. 'You never change, except to get lovelier and lovelier,' he said.

The hallway stretched away from me: a dark tunnel with light at the end where the French windows opened onto the garden at the back. I ran forward. The silver letter tray glimmered on the mahogany table, the ivory knife lying across it like a bone.

'Careful,' my mother called. 'Careful on the rug.'

'Oh let him be,' I heard my uncle saying.

The stairs which led to the distant landing rose beside me. I ran into the living room. The glass top of one of his display cabinets was open. It was full of objects which he had collected on his travels in the East. I stopped and touched a frog, fashioned from smooth, cold, green stone.

'Very precious,' said my uncle coming up behind me.

'What is it?' I asked.

'It's jade,' he said.

The top came down and the catch clicked. 'Very, very precious,' he said.

'Are they all jade?' I pointed at a carved white snake.

'No. Some of them are ivory.'

'What's that?'

'Ivory's from the tusk of an elephant. Jade is a precious stone.'

'Do elephants come from Africa?'

'They can do. These are all African ivory.' He pointed

at the tiny figures, both animal and human lying on the purple velvet.

'Do you know what elephants do when they're dying?' he said, 'they break their tusks, which makes the tusks much less valuable. It's almost as if they don't want us to use them. Now, why don't you go and play outside?'

'Yes,' said my mother from the door. 'You can ask your uncle these questions later.'

I ran past the bowls filled with pot pourri, past the Japanese screen and out into the garden. The grass was spongy beneath my feet. I picked up the badminton racket lying under the net and hit the shuttlecock high into the air. It fell heavily toward me and I hit it again and then again. . . . Later I fetched the pétanque set from the shed and hurled the metal balls at towers of sticks which I constructed.

I was summoned to lunch. The table in the conservatory was covered with a starched white tablecloth which pressed against my legs as I took my place. My uncle insisted that he and my mother drink vodka. Maya poured it from the bottle. It was thick like a liquid syrup.

'To the woman who only ever gets lovelier,' said my uncle.

Their adam's apples bobbed as they swallowed. Maya stood silently watching. The glasses went back on the table. There were finger marks in the glaze of condensation on the side of my mother's glass. Maya moved forward. The thick liquid sounded as it was poured once more.

'And I think a little hock for August today as he's on his own,' said my uncle.

The long necked amber-coloured bottle was lifted out of the ice-filled bucket. Little drops of water ran down the side spattering the table cloth. My hock glass was half-filled.

'Mix it with water,' ordered my mother.

I took the jug and poured some in.

'We don't want you getting drunk today,' she said.

'No, we certainly don't,' said my uncle.

I tasted my wine; it was sweet and watery. Cold soup was ladled from a tureen with a gold rim around the edge into our bowls. The soup was red, tasting of vinegar and garlic. It left an aftertaste like vomit. I said nothing. The bowls were cleared. I was given dark meats that tasted strongly and a salad with walnuts in it. I began to eat. Suddenly I felt a rasping in my chest. I started to cough. My mother slapped me on the back. The coughing went on. My eyes filled with tears. I took a mouthful of hock, but as I tried to swallow it, it spattered out across the table.

'Eat this,' I heard my uncle urging.

'You must,' my mother added.

My mother's earrings were shaking quite near me. I swallowed the ball of dough I had been given. Time seemed to stand still. Then came the feeling in my chest of something moving. I took a breath, shallow and delicate. The pain was gone. I could feel my face cooling rapidly like a coal that falls out of the grate onto the hearth. Through my tear-filled eyes I saw my mother smiling at me.

'Are you all right, darling?' she asked.

I nodded and took another drink of my hock. As the liquid flowed down, it took away the final hurt with it. I put the long-stemmed glass back on the table.

'You should learn to eat more slowly,' I heard my uncle saying.

He was standing on the other side of the table.

'Yes,' I replied meekly.

'Yes – what?' my mother interjected.

'Yes, uncle.'

'And what do you say to your uncle for what he did?'

'Thank you very much, uncle.'

'That's all right,' he said, 'I'm glad I knew what to do.'

'What was it, August?' my mother asked.

'I think it was a piece of walnut,' I said.

'The first time I nearly choked to death I was sailing to Shanghai,' my uncle said. 'I swallowed a fish bone. It was an English steward who showed me the dough trick.'

'When I was nursing,' my mother said, 'we sometimes used to give bread to the patients who had obstructions in their throats.'

'It doesn't surprise me,' said my uncle. 'Much of the best medical practice is based on the simplest principles. In fact it's true of all the sciences.'

My uncle took the hock bottle and replenished my glass.

'Have some more,' he said, 'and listen carefully because I want to give you some advice. When you were choking just now you felt pretty awful, didn't you?'

I nodded.

'You thought you were going to die, didn't you? Well, you weren't. You had at least a couple of minutes' worth of air in your lungs, and if the bread hadn't worked, we'd have turned you upside down and the walnut would have come out of its own accord. So it wasn't as bad as it seemed, was it?'

'No.'

'That's exactly what I'm trying to say. Whenever things seem bad they're never really as bad as they seem. From the inside of the situation, yes, everything always looks totally black. But if you can only step outside it for a moment or two, you'll always see it isn't so bad.'

Uncle Peter tinkled a little bell in the shape of a woman in a long skirt and Maya appeared with a tray of pancakes. My mother lifted two crinkled shapes onto a plate, and squeezed on lemon juice, making the sugar turn colourless.

'There you are August,' she said setting the plate in front of me.

'You molly-coddle that boy,' my uncle muttered. My ears burned red.

'Now, now, now,' I heard my mother saying gently. 'Mother knows best.'

'Mother knows best,' my uncle mocked.

I wanted to look up but I did not dare. I waited for the sound of cutlery on porcelain, picked up my own enormous fork and spoon and began to eat. The pancakes were rubbery. Little bits of sugar stuck to my lips and my chin.

I put down my fork and spoon. My plate was empty.

'Do you feel tired, August?'

It was my mother. I licked the sugar off my lips and the skin round about.

'I'm sure you feel tired, August, you've had all that wine,' she continued.

'I'm sure he must,' chimed my uncle. 'The first time I

had wine, I went out like a light. Like that!' He snapped his fingers.

I looked up. So they wanted me to pretend to be my brother.

'I think I might have a snooze,' I said.

'Come on then. . . .'

My mother led me by the hand into the living room and laid me down on the enormous sofa.

'Do you think you'll have a nice long sleep?' she asked, looking down at me and stroking my forehead.

I liked her attention and pretended to be even more tired than I actually was.

'Mmm . . . yes,' I said, '. . . I think I will. . . .'

I began to drift towards sleep. I could hear my mother and my uncle talking in low tones and laughing together in the garden. The rope of the swing was creaking as she swung backwards and forwards. On the wall there was a picture of a Japanese woman looking over her shoulder. I closed my eyes, turned my head to the side and before very long I was fast asleep. . . .

When I woke up the house was deathly still. I strained my ears for the sound of the creaking rope but I could hear nothing. I felt an ache in my bladder and realised I wanted to pee.

I got up and went out into the hall. Where could everyone be? Then I heard a faint noise. It was Maya upstairs, I decided. But mother and uncle? I told myself they were somewhere. I couldn't believe mother would go without telling me.

I grasped the banister and began to climb. The wood was polished and cool. There was a carpet underfoot held down with brass rods. At the edges the stone showed through. The feel under my feet was solid.

There were more pictures from Japan on the walls. I stopped to look at one. It showed a Japanese woman making a face in a mirror and her infant son who was lying nearby, laughing in response.

The lavatory drew closer. The double doors were open. Sun was streaming through the coloured glass behind. There was the noise again. It sounded like laughter, only lighter. It was coming from beyond the closed door at the other end of the landing. Suddenly I realised. That was

Maya's room. It had to be. Whenever I had sat out in the front garden, it had always been from one of the front windows on the first storey that Maya had looked down. It had to be her making the noise I thought: Maya with her broad face and her watery eyes; her spatula-like fingers; and her heavy boots.

Then it occurred to me that perhaps she would come and play badminton with me. Now that would be something, I thought. I forgot about my pee and started to walk towards the door. I heard the sound again. Yes, it did sound like Maya. She was singing as she combed her hair. She was probably looking down into the front garden and, seeing that it was empty, wondering where I was. Wondering why I wasn't there to wave to. I took hold of the brass handle. It was cold in my hand. Oh yes, it was singing mixed with laughter. It was her all right. Did I knock? No. Not with Maya. There was no need to knock with her. One only knocked on father's study door or at a school master's door. 'Please come and play with me Maya.' I rehearsed the words inwardly. That was how to say it: I turned the handle.

'Hello Maya,' I called.

Throwing open the door, I heard a noise like a shriek and I knew that I had made a terrible mistake.

Uncle was sitting on the bed. Mother was kneeling on the ground between his legs with her head bent forward. My uncle was holding her by the nape of her neck.

'Get out,' I heard my uncle shouting.

I wanted to turn and run but my legs wouldn't move.

'What do you want?' My mother stood up and hurried towards me.

'I was looking for the lavatory,' I stammered.

There was something colourless around her lips. She was wiping it away. On the other side of the room I saw my uncle's eyes were wide with anger, and between his legs I thought I caught a glimpse of something.

'The lavatory's at the end of the landing. You know that perfectly well,' he said.

He turned his back to me and began to button himself up.

'Don't stand there,' said my mother. 'Go on, August.

83

Go to the lavatory. You heard what I said. August, are you listening to me?'

I felt my shoulders being shaken and closed my eyes.

'. . . it's no good trying to be deaf and dumb with me . . . it just won't do. . . . Do you hear?'

I felt two firm slaps on the cheek. I could feel my skin heat up and the pain sting. My eyes filled with tears.

'Let that be a lesson not to play silly games and not to enter without first knocking,' said my mother. 'Do you understand?'

'Yes,' I whispered.

'Yes, what?'

'Yes, mother. . . .'

'Now go to the lavatory. And when you've finished, wash your hands and then go out into the garden and play. Your uncle and I want to be left to talk.'

I turned around, pulling the door shut after myself, and began to walk along the hall. When I was no more than half a dozen paces away I heard a tremendous shout coming from inside the bedroom. It was my uncle. I couldn't tell what he had said but I knew that I was the cause.

I ran into the lavatory, locking the double doors behind. My pee came out in a thick steaming stream and splattered against the side of the bowl. Outside the window the greenery that grew there swayed in the wind and in the distance I could hear children playing.

I grasped the handle and tugged. The water started to cascade with a tremendous noise. I watched with an unwavering stare as it flowed from the edges of the rim and tumbled around at the bottom of the bowl.

There was a clank inside the cistern. The water stopped. I heard the sound of the tank refilling like rain running along a gutter.

I opened the double doors. At the far end of the landing a shaft of sunlight played on the bedroom door still firmly shut. Beyond the wood mother and uncle were having an argument.

I scuttled down the stairs. When I reached the bottom I stopped in my tracks. Mother's and uncle's voices were above me now, fainter but still angry.

I crept down the hall into the living room. Through the

door that led into the conservatory I saw the table had been cleared and laid out for tea. Maya must have done it whilst I had been asleep. Then, when she had finished, she had probably slipped out of the house. I cursed myself for not having noticed this earlier. If I had, I wouldn't have mistaken the noises for Maya. . . .

I went down the two steps and out into the garden. Shadows were lengthening across the grass. I walked over to the swing and sat down. There were children playing nearby, the ones I had already heard. How good to be with them, I thought.

I began to swing myself gently backwards and forwards. The rope creaked. I looked up. It had worn a groove into the bark of the branch above. I touched my face again. It was still tender. Suddenly tears rose up in my eyes and flowed, sticky and salty, down my cheeks.

'Goodbye, August,' said my uncle.

He held out his podgy hand, the gold signet ring a dull band.

'Goodbye, uncle,' I said.

He turned to my mother.

'Goodbye,' she said.

We walked along the hall to the front door which stood waiting open for us.

'Well, until next week,' said my uncle.

'Yes,' replied my mother.

'Let's hope Misha will be better by then. That way August will have someone to play with.'

'He should be,' replied my mother. 'He's only got a mild fever. We'd better be going', she added.

'Yes, you had.'

Uncle Peter gave her a little tap on the shoulder.

'I'm sorry,' she said mysteriously and smiled.

My uncle shrugged his shoulders.

'It can't be helped,' he said. 'Now run along or you'll miss your tram.'

We reached the wooden gate with its Judas hole and tugged it open.

'Wave goodbye to your uncle,' my mother whispered.

I turned around. He was standing at the top of the steps.

'Goodbye,' I called.

He took out his handkerchief and waved it energetically. I could feel his good humour was forced.

'Goodbye, my dears, and safe journey', he called.

'Goodbye. . .' we called back.

We shut the front garden gate and started to walk away along the street. Under the trees hovered swarms of midges; like little grey smudges they were. A storm was brewing. I looked sideways at my mother. She was staring at the ground immediately in front of her.

We reached the corner where we would catch our tram. A couple, arm in arm, were sitting on a low wall, and a man in a green suit with a luxurious handlebar moustache was standing on the kerb. We had left my uncle's early and so there were fewer passengers than usual waiting. Thunder sounded in the distance and it began to grow dark.

The tram curved along the rails towards us, swaying from side to side like a boat. It stopped and we climbed aboard.

'Can we sit at the end?' I asked.

I pointed to the seats at one end which ran across its width.

'Not today,' said my mother. 'I'm tired. I just want to sit down.'

We sat between the doors. The man in the green suit placed himself opposite us. The young couple took the seat which I had wanted and nestled against one another.

Thunder sounded again, like furniture being moved in a room above one's head only louder. The grey sky was split by a silver fork of lightning. It reminded me of the mercury in the bottom of my brother's thermometer. The man in the green suit looked over his shoulder. There was another fork – brighter even than the last. Outside in the street I could see pedestrians looking upwards. The man in the suit turned back towards us and started to stroke his long white moustache.

'Looks like we were just in time,' he said. 'Looks like there's going to be a storm.'

My mother nodded. 'Yes,' she said. 'It does, doesn't it?'

Outside the door the rain started to fall. It made a sus-sus sound like rustling silk. I looked at the pavement. It was covered with big, round wet marks. Thunder clapped overhead – the noise making the heart beat faster – and suddenly, before my eyes, the rain changed from fine needles to thick rods which hit the shoulders of the fleeing pedestrians like water from a hose. A dripping passenger leapt on board. His hair was plastered to his face. He shook himself and drops of water fell onto the floor. There was a damp feeling, just as in winter time.

The bell sounded, and the tram moved off, going faster and faster, until the rails were singing underneath. We lurched around a corner and I was pressed against my mother. She moved away from me as I did, as if flinching from my touch. Was something the matter? I had noticed that the man with the moustache had been looking across. I turned around and stared up at her. She was on my right and she had her left hand over her eyes. One of her long beautiful earrings was shaking. I reached out and tugged at her hand.

'Mother,' I said. 'Are you all right?'

She dropped her hand slightly. I saw that her eyes were filled with wetness.

'Please leave me alone,' she whispered.

I tried to touch her arm but she shrugged it away. Her whole body was shaking. She was sobbing. I could hear it quite distinctly above the rattle of the tram and I began to feel embarrassed. I turned to face the front again. The man with the moustache raised his index finger to me and shook it from side to side in a forbidding way. I gazed at the window. It was covered with drops of rain. Outside the city passed in a blur.

When we alighted at our stop, it was still pouring with rain. We huddled in the doorway of a draper's shop with a headless mannequin in the window.

Finally, the storm died down, and the rain dwindled to a fine drizzle. We started to walk towards home. There were puddles everywhere and in the gutters the water seemed to be singing as it flowed along. I remembered the illustration from my Hans Christian Andersen book of the little tin soldier sailing off down the street in a paper boat in search of his lady love, the ballerina from the top of the music box.

We stopped in front of a furniture shop.

'Why have you stopped?' I asked.

'Hold this, will you?' she replied quietly handing me the small clutch handbag which she used on Sundays. It was made of black jet.

She peered at the large mirror of the dressing table that was on display and I saw reflected back an anxious face with hair coming undone at the back. She moistened her fingers and ran them along her eyebrows.

'Do I look all right?' she asked.

I looked into the street. For the first time in my life it occurred to me that the atmosphere of that particular hour on a Sunday was sad. A night's sleep away lay the first day of the working week and everyone knew it.

'Why don't you use the mirror in your bag?' I asked.

There were boys from our neighbourhood approaching on the other side of the street. I didn't want them to see me holding her handbag.

'Do I look all right?' she repeated.

'Here's your handbag,' I said.

'You're no use at all,' she muttered, running her hands through her hair.

'Yes I am,' I piped. 'You do look very nice.'

'Yes, of course you are.' She turned and, much to my relief, took the handbag.

We approached the door of our apartment block. I saw the porter standing outside, in his pea-green coat, slightly faded, with gold epaulettes on the shoulders. He was smoking his funny silver pipe with its silver hood.

As he saw us coming he put it away. He wasn't meant to smoke on the job and sometimes the older tenants used to complain about the smell of his tobacco. We drew level with him and he opened the door.

'Good evening, Mrs Slemic,' he said.

'Good evening,' she replied.

'Bad storm. I hope you weren't caught out in it.'

'No. We were on the tram at the time.'

'There's flooding, you know, in some parts of the city. . . .'

We walked down the carpeted hall, past the enormous gilt mirror and the two armchairs which no one ever sat in with the two imitation Greek vases on the shelf above, and stepped into the lift. The porter behind us shut one and then the other of the grille gates with a crash. My mother pressed the button marked five with a gloved finger. We began to rise.

'God, that man is so irritating,' she said. 'As if we weren't aware that it hadn't rained. . . !'

I heard the sound of the cable turning far above me and felt the lightness in my stomach which I always experienced in the lift.

She put her finger under my chin and lifted my face.

'What are you going to say about today when your brother and father ask you about it?' she said.

'I don't know,' I replied, although I did know perfectly well. She was talking about uncle and the bedroom.

She removed her finger. At the side of my left leg I could feel the velvet of the seat cushion.

'Well. What are you going to say?'

'I'll say it was a bit lonely without Misha,' I said, 'and that next Sunday I hope he'll be well enough to come with me. . . .'

I knew that I had said the right thing. She reached forward and stroked the back of my head.

'Good boy,' she said.

My right hand was around my left wrist. Suddenly, I could quite distinctly feel it through the ends of my fingers. It was my pulse, slowly, patiently, unfailingly beating away, exactly as my mother had described it to me.

Later that evening I lay in bed with my face to the wall. I heard the sound of my mother's footsteps and the door opening.

'August,' she called quietly, 'are you still awake?'

'Yes,' I mumbled.

With the fingertips of my right hand I could feel my pulse beating underneath. All that evening I had been doing the trick to reassure myself that I hadn't lost the knack.

'Dear, darling, beloved August,' she whispered, 'your mother loves you more than anyone else in the world. You know, don't you darling? And she didn't mean to do what happened today, she didn't mean to slap you. You know that, don't you, darling. . . ?'

I mumbled agreement and closed my eyes.

She began to stroke my forehead with her firm hands and continued.

'Dear August, darling August. . . .'

I felt her wedding ring on my skin and became aware that she was crying. But I didn't look or speak. I was tired and nothing was better than to fall asleep with her somewhere nearby.

After that, Sundays at my uncle's became quite different. Quite suddenly, my father started to come, unhappy in his always too-tight-fitting suits. The meals didn't seem to be the same fun as those we had enjoyed when it had been just my brother and my mother and myself, and I noticed that the food changed. Gone was the grey caviar in little white dishes shaped like lids and the herrings that tasted bitter-sweet, and in their places appeared sausages and coarse pâtés, which you could buy at any corner delicatessen and which was the sort of food I was used to at home. The after-dinner routine changed as well. Instead of my brother being put to sleep for half an hour on the sofa, and I being allowed to wander around the house and garden, he would be allowed to stay up, and he, my mother and I, at her insistence, would play together, badminton or pétanque, neither of which she had ever shown the remotest interest in before. She did this as she made a point of saying, so that my father and uncle, 'the brothers' as she had started calling them, could be left alone in the conservatory with their hock and their vodka to discuss politics, economics and other important subjects.

Gradually our visits became less frequent: we would miss the odd Sunday here and there, and we started to leave after lunch without waiting for tea. Then my father bought a car and we began to go even less, as we had the excuse that we were exploring the countryside, or

90

using the car to visit other relatives who lived further afield. Finally, when I was twelve, we stopped going altogether and I thereafter would only see my uncle at Christmas and at New Year and at the large family gatherings which occasionally took place.

The next time I went to where my uncle lived I was eighteen. It was a June day, warm but windy, with big white clouds scudding across the sky. In a few weeks I would be on my way to England and I wanted to make his acquaintance again and say 'Goodbye'. I was aware that things were going wrong in Europe and that it might be a long time before I saw him again, if at all.

The tram which I caught out rattled and creaked; the bell, when I pulled the stirrup, tinkled faraway: and when Maya opened the door, her eyes were as green as ever. As I walked across the paved front garden, memories came flooding back. The ornamental cherry trees were in flower beside me and white and pink petals lay on the ground. The front door at the top of the stairs was open. I suddenly expected my uncle to appear with his round, hot face, mopping his brow and exclaiming, 'Welcome, a thousand times welcome. . . .'

I stopped at the bottom and waited for Maya to catch up with me.

'Where's uncle?' I asked when she drew close.

'He's in the garden,' she replied. 'You'll find him very changed. We're none of us getting any younger, you know. . . .'

I stepped from the living room into the garden. My uncle was sitting in a deck chair, sunning himself, with someone sitting close by him.

He rose stiffly and turned to look at me. His suit was hanging from bony shoulders and his face was gaunt with the cheekbones showing through. Every bit of flesh seemed to have gone from his body. Only his eyes were alive.

He held out his hand. He no longer wore the signet ring on his now very thin little finger.

'My dear August, how nice to see you,' he said.

I gazed over his shoulder at the figure sitting in the other deck chair, a young girl with long reddish hair.

'Ah August . . .' he said, 'you must meet my help-mate, Zara. . . .'

He squeezed my arm and gave me a knowing wink.

'. . . Zara. . . . Come here. . . .'

Zara stood up. I saw that she had been eating a lemon sorbet out of a fluted glass and that there was a streak of sorbet on the side of her cheek. She came towards me, wiping it away, and I remembered how my mother had risen and come towards me, wiping her mouth, all those years before. As we shook hands. I noticed that Zara was wearing uncle's signet ring on her marriage finger.

After lunch we sat in the garden together, my uncle and myself. We talked of my mother who had been buried nine months before. My uncle wept, big tears spilling down the parchment-like skin of his face.

'I loved her. I loved your mother,' he said, over and over again.

I nodded and said that I understood.

Later, we took a little walk, something we had never done before, through the leafy, suburban streets around his villa, my uncle's arm linked through mine, his frail body pressing against me, and his bamboo cane tap-tap-tapping along the pavement.

Somewhere along the way he stopped.

'I want to give you some advice,' he said.

He turned to look at me and waved in the direction of the villa.

'Always have a sweetheart,' he said, 'and don't listen to what other people say about it. They'll say it's wrong. They'll say that you're too old or too young. They'll say you're leading her astray. They'll think of something. But don't listen to them. Look at me. I'm dying and I'm going to go out of this unhappy world with a smile on my face.'

A number of images passed through my mind one after the other. I saw my uncle, red-faced, looking at me across the lunch table as I choked on my walnut; the Japanese print of the woman looking into the mirror to amuse her baby; my mother on the floor before my uncle, turning to look at me with an expression of outrage. The memories came in a rush and brought with them a feeling of nausea.

I ran behind the tree and was sick. My vomit came out with great ease, as if my body was expelling something it was longing to be rid of. Afterwards I looked at it as it lay like a yellow puddle on the earth and I noticed that I felt no taste in my throat.

When I went back to my uncle he was standing where I had left him. He was leaning on his stick and staring at the ground. He hadn't noticed my absence. I took him by the arm and we walked on in silence.

Travelling home on the tram, I reflected on what had happened. How could my mother have done what she had done? An adolescent anger took hold of me. It started as a small hardness and grew steadily bigger and stronger.

By the time I reached home I had determined that I would not visit my mother's grave before I left Warsaw, and to my undying shame I did not, nor have I visited it since.

1981:
Evening

The doorbell rang – two short rings.

In the cloakroom I was looking in the mirror above the washbasin at my coconut-shaped head and my grey eyes with white rims around the edges. I pulled the linen hand-towel from the bar under the sink and began to dry my hands. There was a smell of lavender soap and beyond the narrow window I could hear birds singing in the garden. It was the sound of a suburban summer's evening: shrill, and at the same time melancholy.

'Will you answer the door, August?' Eunice's voice drifted up from the basement.

Whenever the bell went, or for that matter the telephone, Eunice was invariably somewhere else and I was always the one to anwser it. It was a gift she had – like always winning raffles – another of her talents.

I folded the damp towel and draped it over the bar.

'Okay, I'm going,' I shouted down.

I pulled the door of the cloakroom and began to walk along the hall. Outside the front door Damian drummed his fingers on the wood, as he always did when he came.

'I'm coming,' I shouted.

I passed the living room on my right, stretching the whole depth of the house. Sun was slanting through the front window and across the floor.

I rounded the corner and stepped into the vestibule. It smelt of rubber from the waterproofs hanging on the coat-rack.

The electronic latch sprang open when I touched it and I pulled back the door. Damian was standing on the steps in a blue suit and a dark silk tie held in place with a gold bar.

'Hi, Pop! What kept you?'

He took a puff of the cigarette which he was smoking and threw it down.

'I was drying my hands.'

The glowing butt lay on the green paving stones.

'Couldn't you have thrown it away inside?' I asked.

'Bio-degradable,' replied Damian.

My son's face was long with dark eyes set far back under a bony forehead and a large nose jutting out over a small mouth. The overall impression of his appearance was of bone coming to a point.

'Am I coming in?' he asked.

I saw that Damian was making one of his expressions. It was a quizzical look which he used in all sorts of situations. I would have been hard-pressed to say exactly what the look implied, but it had an edge of danger to it.

'Why don't you ever use the key which we gave you?' I asked.

'I thought it was just for emergencies.'

Damian brushed past me and stopped on the huge doormat, which he had given us, just inside.

'Well it's your house too you know. We gave you that key so that you could come and go as you pleased.'

'Appreciate the thought, Pop! Really I do,' drawled Damian in a fake American accent.

I shut the door and Damian began to wipe his feet in an exaggerated manner on the doormat. A fine brown dust rose from the pile with a smell which reminded me of rope. 'I don't want to bring any filth into the house, partner.'

'Your mat was a great present,' I lied.

Damian darted away into the hall. I tugged the front door to make certain it was shut properly and went after him. When I turned the corner I saw my son was standing in the doorway of the sun-filled living room.

'Well, it never changes,' said Damian, clapping his hands. 'Day to day, month to month, year to year – it's just the same as it always was. How are you, Pop, and how's the mother?' he asked.

'I'm fine,' I replied, 'and I think your mother's fine as well.'

'Think! You think the mother's well. . . ? You mean to say you don't know. . . .' He turned and disappeared into the living room. 'I'm not interested in what you think! I'm not interested in what you think! I'm interested in facts, Dummkopf!'

'Of course I'm all right,' came Eunice's voice from the basement. 'Of course I'm all right.'

'Hi, Mum,' Damian shouted from inside.

I stepped into the room after my son. It was long, with windows at either end, two fire-places of black marble and large old Chinese tea-drums filled with pot pourri standing in each corner.

'And how are you?' I asked my son.

Damian, at the little papier-mâché table, was winding the key at the back of the gilded birdcage which rested on top.

'Oh I'm pretty well today. . . .' He moved the flat brass lever at the bottom.

'I sold two Zanussi washing machines and God knows how many microwave ovens.'

The mechanical bird on the perch inside began to open and close its beak whilst an imitation twittering and warbling rose up from below.

'Which for a Tuesday I can tell you ain't bad,' continued Damian.

'Do you get commission?'

'Of course I get commission.'

Damian skirted the back of the chintz-covered sofa to the other occasional table, and lifted the lid of the cigarette box which rested on top.

'It wouldn't be worth my while, otherwise, would it?' he continued.

The music box mechanism released by the lid began to tinkle out 'The Blue Danube'.

Damian took a cigarette and picked up the lighter from the mantelpiece.

'Oh yes. After I deliver the second Zanussi to Mrs Gore at seven-thirty,' he whirled the flint, '. . . I shall be having a few celebratory beers with the boys on the strength of my commission.' He lifted the flame to the end of his cigarette and inhaled.

The clock on the mantelpiece began to sound six o'clock, its chimes clear and glasslike, joined a moment later by the sonorous booms of the grandfather clock which stood in the hall at the bottom of the stairs. In its cage the twittering bird had begun to flap its wings and the slow, sad version of 'The Blue Danube' trickled on.

I thought it was typical of my son to have made an arrangement which would require him to leave almost immediately, and also typical that Damian should have revealed his plans in such an off-hand way.

'Why couldn't Mrs Gore have her washing machine on Thursday?' I asked.

Damian lifted back the two metal balls hanging from the end of the Newton's Cradle. A moment later two metal balls at the other end flew away in the opposite direction.

'The lady wants it tonight – she gets it tonight,' said Damian.

I heard footfalls in the hallway. I turned and saw Eunice coming through the door. She clicked across the parquet towards me. She was wearing a plastic apron with a vast Lea & Perrins bottle on the front.

'Gosh what a lot of noise,' exclaimed Eunice. 'I can barely hear myself think. . . .'

The caged bird warbled tinnily and stopped: 'The Blue Danube' slowed to a funereal pace: and the sound of the Newton's Cradle died to a faint clack. The clocks had finished striking.

'That's better,' said Eunice. She undid the apron at the back and walked towards Damian by the fireplace.

'Nice to see you, darling boy,' she said. 'How are you?'

I watched as my son, holding his cigarette at arm's length, bent his thin body forward and received Eunice's full kisses on his cheeks.

'Scuse the appearance,' said Eunice in a mock-cockney accent, as she stepped back. 'But mother's been in the kitchen making her favourite boy his favourite cold carrot soup.'

I looked down at the caged bird on the table. A false

tongue had been painted on the fabric stretched across its throat.

'I don't think Damian can join us,' I said.

'Going to miss mother's chilled carrot soup. Oh no,' wailed Eunice. 'But for why?'

She threw her plastic apron onto the sofa where it landed with a dull rubbery thud.

'I've got to deliver a washing machine,' Damian said.

'He's really only got half an hour,' I interjected.

'Oh no!' Eunice widened her eyes. 'But you'll have a drink anyway? Won't you?'

'Oh yes. Never known to refuse a drink,' said Damian.

Eunice put her arm in his and began to walk towards the back of the room with him.'

'Your visits are always too short,' I heard Eunice saying behind me in her imitation baby voice, ' . . . and you know, your poor old parents, we do love you. . . .'

'Why, of course you do. . . .' Damian made his standard reply in his false American accent.

'What'll you have to drink?' I asked from the drinks table.

'I think I'll have. . . .' Damian stared at the table. It had once been on a ship, and around the edges there were hinged flaps. Eunice and I had bought it shortly after our honeymoon one damp Saturday afternoon in the Portobello Road. It was the first piece of furniture we had bought together.

'What are you having, Pops?' I heard Damian asking.

'I think I'm going to have a whisky,' I replied.

'Oh yes. I think a whisky would be a very good idea,' said Eunice. 'A long cool one.'

'Then I'll have a whisky too,' said Damian.

I picked up the bottle of Bells.

'It's a pity you have to go, Damian,' I said. 'I was going to ask you a little favour.'

I tipped the bottle and began to pour. The liquid was pale and smelt sourly.

'Did you hear what I said about the little favour?' I repeated.

'We're waiting with bated breath,' said Damian.

'It's about the clock radio.'

'Oh no, not the clock radio,' moaned Damian. 'Not that bloody thing again.'

'It's still tuned to that wretched news programme,' I said quietly, 'and I can't get it to play classical music in the morning.'

'Oh, give the poor boy a break,' I heard Eunice saying at my side. 'He's been looking after old ladies and their broken electric kettles all day, and come evening the last thing he wants to do is fiddle around with father's clock radio.'

'I was only asking,' I said. 'It's not a crime, is it?'

I picked up the ice tongs with the arms of the island of Jersey enamelled on the end.

'Why don't you bring it in to Damian in the shop one day?' advised Eunice.

'Bring it into me in the shop. That's a great idea,' said Damian.

Why won't he just do it? I thought to myself.

I sighed. 'Yes, okay. I'll bring it up to the shop,' I said sullenly.

'Pop, please don't be like that, do you hear me?'

I turned, feelings of dread and anger mingling in my stomach. I looked at Damian but, instead of the sallow-skinned young man with a long nose and bony forehead whom I had greeted at the front door a few minutes earlier, I now saw two dark angry eyes.

'I said I'll do it and I will,' Damian continued, carefully enunciating each of his words. 'But in the meantime just stop nagging me about it.'

'Yes,' said Eunice, 'you're always nagging. You must stop it.'

'I'm not nagging. I was just asking,' I said. 'It is seven months since Christmas and it's not a very remarkable request to make of one's son who works in a shop that sells electrical goods, that he comes and looks at one of the appliances that came from his own shop and fixes it.'

'Hush, hush,' said Eunice, looking at me directly. 'He's only been here two minutes and already it looks as though there's going to be a full-scale row.'

'No row is going to erupt,' I said irritably. 'You're being over-dramatic as usual.'

Inside, I felt an overwhelming desire to throw over the table.

'I was just making a perfectly simple request.' I went on, 'and don't tell me to "Hush, hush . . ." either.'

'All right, I won't' said Eunice. She looked at me and smiled sweetly. She had an ability to suddenly become charming in disagreeable situations which always disarmed me.

'Now, what about our drinkies?' continued Eunice. 'I don't know about you two, but I'm thirsty.'

She took the tongs from me and lifted the lid off the ice-bucket.

'Oh God,' she exclaimed. 'There's no ice. Would you be a lovey, August? I meant to bring it up but I forgot. It's in the bowl on the kitchen table.'

I fetched the ice and returned. We took our glasses and went and sat down. As we drank Damian and Eunice talked but I was mainly silent. I was sulking. When he had finished Damian looked at his watch and said he had to go. 'Absolutely,' I said. I wanted him to leave as quickly as possible.

He said goodbye to his mother and I followed him out to the vestibule. I opened the front door and he stepped out.

'Be seeing you, Pop,' he said. Damian had one foot on the first step and his hand on the railing.

'Listen, about your clock-radio,' he continued. 'I have to rush today, but next week when I come I'll do it for you. Okay?'

I wanted to shout at him but I could not think what. I smelt whisky on my son's breath.

'Bye, Mom,' he called back through the open door.

'Bye, dearest,' drifted back her reply.

'See you, Pop.'

Damian punched me affectionately on the shoulders with his clenched fist.

'Break a leg, as they say.'

He pounded down the steps two at a time and struck out across the paving stones for the gate. His speed reminded me of my own youth and the way that I, in my time, had fled from my parents.

'Goodbye,' I called after him frigidly.

Damian opened the gate, gave a cursory wave and stepped out. It shut behind him with a dull thud. Fragments of dried green paint fell to the ground and lay there like sprinkles of confetti.

I watched Damian moving away. My son's hair was dark, bluish almost, and curly. Inside myself I could feel my hardness and my anger towards him loosening and dissolving. It always disappeared just when it was too late.

I stood trying to make out the sound of Damian's footsteps, but all I could hear were young children splashing about in a paddling pool in a neighbour's garden. At the back of my throat I felt the ache tugging. It was the same as the feeling I used to get as a boy when my parents left me to go out to dinner. Or when Rita was angry with me. Or when I lost something and could not find it.

I looked up at the sky. It was pale, the colour of cornflowers with thin lines of cloud lying across it. Why was it always the same pattern, I wondered? of anger and then ache? Why could I never learn to escape it? It was like being bound to a wheel which went round and round, on and on.

'Has he gone?' Eunice shouted.

'Yes of course he's gone,' I muttered. 'Of course he's bloody gone.'

'What did you say?' Eunice shouted back.

'Oh it doesn't matter,' I called.

I stepped into the vestibule and shut the door. The noise echoed through the house.

'No need to slam the door,' called Eunice.

A coat had fallen from its hook and lay in a heap. It was a Burberry with grease stains on the front. I hardly wore it any more. I hung it up and went into the hall shouting ahead, 'Why didn't you tell me to mind the paintwork like you usually do when I slam the door?'

I stopped in front of the living room.

Eunice pushed a needle through a hole in her embroidery round and lifted it high, pulling a length of off-white yarn after it.

'Oh be quiet, you old fuss pot,' Eunice replied.

'And why didn't you bloody well help me when I asked him to fix my clock-radio?'

'You're like a needle stuck in the groove of a record,' she said.

'If that's your attitude. I don't want to bloody well go to Peggy's party with you,' I said.

I turned and walked away down the hall. I noticed a grubby hand mark on the second door into the living room which we never used.

'And I don't want to bloody well go with you to Peggy's either,' she called after me.

'Well, that settles it,' I shouted back. 'I'm bloody going on my own.'

I wrenched open the cloakroom door and stepped inside. It smelt of lavatory disinfectant mixed with perfume. Eunice's bottle of Chanel stood on the window ledge. She had put it on specially for Damian's visit.

'What were you doing in the vestibule for so long?' called Eunice.

'What?' I said mechanically. My urine trickled out.

'What were you doing in the vestibule?'

I pulled the lavatory chain. Water gushed down and began to turn round and round.

'Are you listening?' Eunice called.

'Hanging a coat,' I replied.

'Fibber,' shouted Eunice from the front room. 'You were up to some mischief. I know you.'

I came out into the hall. Why the probing and questioning? Why the accusation of imaginary crimes?

'And now you're up to some mischief in the hall,' she said.

'Are you coming to the party or aren't you?'

I addressed her through the open doorway of the living room.

'No I am not. I wouldn't be seen dead in public with you.'

'Eunice, don't be like that.'

'I'm not being like anything. I'm just being myself.'

'You'll enjoy yourself.'

'I don't want to come.'

'Peggy will miss you.'

'I don't care. Peggy can miss me all she likes.'

'You're only like this because of Damian coming and going and never having any time for us.'

She went on working at her tapestry.

'What is it Eunice? Why are we like this?'

She looked up and stared at me directly.

'To tell you the truth, I do not know, dear August. It must be the nerves.'

'We used to be happy once.'

'We used to be happy once, that's true.'

'And now we're not happy any more and everything we do seems to rub the other person up the wrong way.'

'But we get along, don't we?' she said. 'If we didn't have each other, it would be worse, wouldn't it? Think of being all alone in this big old house. I often think of it and it gives me the shivers. Think of getting up every morning and no one to say "Good morning" to. Think of coming home every evening and no one to say "Good evening" to. We have our ups and downs but we're also the best companions each of us has. Isn't that right?'

I went behind Eunice, bent forward and kissed her on her forehead. Her skin smelt of powder.

'Eunice is August's little girl, isn't she?'

'Yes,' I murmured.

'And she always will be?'

'Of course, darling. Your tapestry is coming along nicely.'

She held it at arm's length. The scene was set in a wood. A clown in an old-fashioned costume sat playing the guitar with a sad expression on his face. Great dark oaks towered overhead and in a corner, on a pedestal, stood a naked statue of Venus, her back half-turned towards him.

'I think it's from a famous painting,' said Eunice, 'but God knows which one. My memory's getting like a sieve.'

Then she added. 'We really should go to the art galleries one day. Here we are, living in London, world centre of culture, and all we do is sit at home.'

I kissed her on the forehead again.

'Are you sure you're not going to come?'

'Sure I'm sure. I'd rather stay. I'll watch the Royal fireworks on the television. But you go. You'll enjoy it.'

'You're only saying that.'

'I promise you I'm not. You know me. Greta Garbo the second. "I want to be a-lone." '

I rose, my knees creaking.

'I am getting old,' I said. 'Another drink?'

Eunice took my hand and began to jig it up and down in hers.

'Love me?'

'Yes, I love you,' I said.

'I'd love a drink,' she said. 'And lots of water in the whisky, otherwise you'll see me tipsy,' she recited. 'Dearest August.'

I imagine that after he left his parents' house in Chiswick, Damian went straight to a pub in the Abbey Road. A young woman in a white dress with a prominent label was sitting outside. Her name was Ruth.

'How did it go?' Ruth asked as he sat down.

'God, it was a nightmare,' said Damian. 'I had to tell them I was working. I thought I'd never get away. The old man even asked me to fix his fucking clock-radio again. I wish I'd never given it to him.'

'Aren't you going to kiss me?' she said, leaning forward with her eyes closed and pursing her lips.

I could hear the noise from Peggy's party as I walked down the street. From the quality of the laughter I judged there would be few guests under thirty.

I opened the gate and looked down the path. On the wall under the porch sat a young couple holding their heads together.

'What do you want to do?' I heard the young man asking the girl. There was something mysterious on his tee-shirt.

'I want to open a radio station in Alaska and play my favourite pop songs,' she said.

She lifted up her bare legs and curled her toes. The nails were the colour of holly berries, the same as her red mouth.

'I'll be your DJ then,' said the young man.

107

'Oh no you won't,' she said firmly. 'There'll just be me.'

I approached and the youth looked up. His spiky hair was shiny.

'Hello,' I greeted, although I had no idea who they were. 'Why aren't you enjoying the party?'

'We're here to keep out gate-crashers.' The young man threw his cigarette down and stubbed it out. His shoes were pointed and tied at the side.

'Have there been any gate-crashers?' I enquired.

'Where there's a party there are always gate-crashers,' said the young man. 'It's a rule of nature.'

The figures on his tee-shirt were naked cowboys with penises like gigantic lengths of hose-pipe.

'August. . . .' I heard a woman calling.

Peggy was standing in the doorway in what looked like Nigerian national costume.

'I see you've spotted Jonathan's ghastly tee-shirt.' Peggy swayed as she spoke. 'I have promised him that if I see that thing lying around, I shall burn it.'

'Hello Peggy,' I said.

I took her hand.

'Hello`August, so nice that you could come.'

I brushed her rouged cheek with my lips.

'Aparently there's even a tee-shirt with a picture of Her Majesty sitting on the lavatory or so I was told. Absolutely disgusting,' she said.

Around her freckled neck she wore a heavy silver necklace. It was made out of a series of crudely cut squares and crescents. There was a large turquoise pendant at the bottom.

'And where is Mrs Slemic, may a hostess ask?'

'She couldn't come,' I explained. 'She sends her apologies.'

'Oh no, but this is too disappointing. I was so looking forward to seeing little Eunice.'

'She's got a touch of the 'flu.'

My face reddened and I was glad that we were moving. It had saved me lying to Peggy's face. We turned the corner and the inner hallway opened up in front of us.

'You haven't seen the new kitchen, have you?' exclaimed Peggy.

'No, I haven't.'

'Here! Take this!'

She handed me her glass; a length of lemon peel was stuck to the side.

'Parties – I don't know why I do them,' she said. 'They're sheer hell.'

She lifted her dress and began to descend the basement stairs unsteadily in her silver sling-backs.

'Follow me.'

I stepped forward gingerly. The stairs were covered – like everywhere on the ground floor – with a protective hessian which looked treacherous.

A man in a white coat flitted past the bottom.

'Patrice,' called Peggy, gripping the banister.

The man in the white coat reappeared. His forehead was large and white.

'Are they enjoying themselves outside?'

Patrice pulled at the cuffs of his white gloves.

'Very much, Madame.'

'Thank you, Patrice. Are you behind me, August?'

'I am.'

'There's a serious danger I'm going to topple.'

I put my hand on her shoulder.

'This bloody stuff on the carpets everywhere. I hate it. Makes the house like an ice-rink. But Jeremy said we had to have it.'

'People do behave very strangely with cigarettes in other people's houses,' I observed.

'Like bloody animals, which is why Jeremy is right.'

A clicking sound from Peggy's heels announced she had reached the bottom. A moment later I felt solidity beneath my own feet.

'I hope you're not going to find my new kitchen a dreadful bore.'

'I'm sure I won't,' I replied.

'Along with dreams, other people's home improvements are the most boring things in the world, aren't they?' she said.

Four doors led off from the basement hallway. A newspaper photograph of the King and Queen of Spain was sellotaped to one of them.

'Isobel, the cook's – she's a monarchist,' explained Peggy.

She took back her glass and drained the final dregs from the bottom.

'Empty! Patrice. . . . Refill for Madame . . .' she shrieked.

We moved towards an open door. In the room beyond I glimpsed a refrigerator, gleaming saucepans and shining white worktops. More of the slippery protective sheeting covered the floor and there was a woman on a stool.

Suddenly I became aware of Peggy pushing me back with her hand.

'. . . August . . .' Peggy whispered. 'There's a very very good friend of mine in there called Marjorie. She's very very sad and I want you to be very nice to her. Will you do that for me?'

'Yes.'

'Just divorced. A bit shaky.'

I nodded.

She took me by the arm and led me in.

Through the basement window I could see the ankles and the feet of the guests out on the lawn.

'Marjorie,' exclaimed Peggy. Her dress billowed as she swept forward. 'Fancy sitting down here on your ownsome.'

Marjorie, sitting at the breakfast counter, swivelled around.

'I'm repairing the ravages of time,' she said.

She lifted the tiny mirror she was holding and ran the mascara pencil along her eyelid.

'Are you enjoying yourself?' asked Peggy.

The compact which held the mirror clicked shut.

'I'm still waiting for those introductions to those gorgeous hulks which you promised me.'

Marjorie glanced at me. Her fair hair was held in place with a velvet headband. Her lips were thickly covered with dark red lipstick.

'. . . Marjorie . . .' Peggy took Marjorie's arm. 'I want you to meet my dear friend. . . .'

I grasped Marjorie's extended hand. A lucky charm bracelet jingled around her wrist.

'This is August Slemic,' said Peggy.

'How do you do,' I said.

'And I'm Marjorie Wingate, the merry divorcee. Very pleased to meet you,' she said.

I looked into her broad face. Behind the make-up I sensed it was flushed with drink. She was in her forties.

'I'm parched.' Peggy struck her glass with a knife.

'Patrice,' she shouted.

From a door Patrice emerged, holding something in a cloth. There was a low popping sound and he produced a bottle of champagne.

'Bravo,' called Peggy.

She took the lemon peel out of her glass and hurled it towards the sink. It landed six feet away on the side of the extractor above the cooker.

'We women are such useless shots,' giggled Peggy.

'That's because that's what we've been brought up to be,' said Marjorie.

Peggy shook her head violently at her friend.

'Haven't I told you to stop that women's lib nonsense?' said Peggy.

'You did,' said Marjorie. 'You're quite right.'

Their bodies drooped forward until their foreheads were touching. They put their arms around one another's shoulders.

'I love you,' said Marjorie.

'And I love you too, dear pal,' said Peggy. 'Aren't we a pair of pathetic old drunks?'

I held out the glass I had been given and waited as the champagne was poured.

Patrice had removed his gloves to reveal long finger-nails with dirt below.

'Thank you,' I said.

The waiter bowed slightly and moved on to the women.

'Drinkies . . . splash it in . . .' cried Peggy as she and Marjorie held out their glasses.

'Up to the top. We're all going to get plastered. And have one yourself, Patrice.'

He wiped the end of the champagne bottle with the white cloth he was carrying over his other arm.

'Thank you, Madame. Later.' His voice was booming and sonorous. 'When the hurly-burly's done.' I guessed he had been on the stage.

111

Patrice glided off, the bottle held in front of him like a spear.

'Well, here's to you both,' said Peggy. 'And to no more women's lib. It's a load of rot, isn't it, August? I've told her she'll never get a man if she talks like that. It's true, isn't it, August?'

'I suppose it's true,' I replied.

'Thank you, thank you,' bellowed Peggy. 'A true answer at last. I propose a toast to August who always tells the truth. Don't you, my dear boy?'

She lifted her glass, slopping champagne on her hand.

'Yes, to August, the last gentleman in the world,' I heard Marjorie saying.

I turned and saw she too was holding her glass held high.

'You're damned good looking,' said Marjorie. 'Isn't he Peggy?'

'Damned good looking,' echoed Peggy.

'. . . To August. . . .'

We clinked glasses and a moment later I felt the first taste of champagne on my tongue, fizzy and cold and to my mind tasting ever so faintly of mouldering corks.

'Why's he so good looking?' It was Marjorie speaking.

'Because he's a Pole,' explained Peggy.

'You're a Pole?' There was a crescent of lipstick on Marjorie's glass with lines running across it.

'Yes, I am a Pole,' I answered, 'but I left a long time ago.'

'You're a Pole and I'm a Jew,' she exclaimed. 'We should make a fabulous conjunction. Have you got a car, Mr August?'

'God, she's a fast one,' giggled Peggy.

In the garden behind I saw a pair of women's legs and the moving hem of a black skirt. Everything was happening more quickly than I had expected. I felt a vague sense of excitement in my stomach at the thought of the mildly dangerous act I was about to perform.

'Yes,' I said. 'I do have a car.'

'Will you give me a lift home later?'

'Of course he will,' boomed Peggy. 'Now come on, you two. It's time to circulate. We've got fireworks soon. You

112

can't leave until then. Tomorrow's the big day. Prince C. is going to put one into Lady Di's oven.'

'Oh, you are horrible,' giggled Marjorie to her friend.

I followed the women out the door and climbed the metal stairs that led up to the garden. As we stepped onto the grass I glimpsed Patrice amongst the bushes at the far end, nailing a Catherine Wheel to a wooden trellis.

There would be fireworks, there would be drinking, and later I was going to take Marjorie home.

December 30th 1980

Today is Tuesday. Last night when I travelled home the Tube was practically empty. At the other end of the carriage there was a man carrying a large flagon of cider who was sick on the floor. At Paddington a passenger fetched a guard. The man with the cider jar was asked to leave. I thought there was going to be a scene but the man agreed to go without making any difficulties.

He rose unsteadily to his feet. 'Happy Christmas, everyone,' he said.

'Yes, all right,' said the guard.

'And a herpes-filled New Year,' continued the man.

None of the passengers responded. Swinging his cider bottle the man stepped through the door, waved at some of us through the window and walked away.

The guard poured sand from a fire bucket on the vomit. When he had finished he came over and said, 'I don't know! Why can't we enjoy ourselves any more without making a mess of things?'

This morning it was busier coming in to work and there was a great deal of talk amongst the passengers about Christmas presents received and the forthcoming sales. Here at Slemic and Co. it is fairly quiet. My only task today will be to show someone around a house in Bloomsbury at midday.

My notebook is filling up. I looked at the finished pages proudly just as I once used to look at my essay books at school. These are some events from my later life arranged in chronological order.

* * *

On arriving in London I was overawed and overwhelmed by the noise of the motor cars and the old open-topped buses. They roared outside the window of my hotel like the sea. It was so different from home where I was used to the screeching trams and, nearer at hand, the cycle of the lift: the double grille doors shutting one after the other; the sound of the clutch engaging and the wheel beginning to turn; the sus-sus of the lift rising and falling; and finally the clatter as the grille doors opened and shut once again.

The only variation to this pattern of noises was when the night bell was rung after the doors were locked. Whenever I heard it sounding as a child I would always picture the same figure on the steps: a good-looking young man in his twenties wearing spats, with a top hat slightly askew on his head. After I grew older, the bell sounding in the darkness continued to conjure up the same image. In London that first night, the possibilities for this sort of dreaming were that much greater, and all night long fantasies which seemed to grow out of the traffic kept me half-awake. I re-lived the journey I had just made by train and boat from Poland, but every detail was exaggerated and grotesque. The next morning when I went down to breakfast I was too tired to eat.

During my first year at Leeds I made friends with one of the University lecturers: Mr Longhorn. When the summer of 1939 came round, Mr Longhorn invited me to accompany him and his family on their annual summer holidays to Cornwall. It did not seem advisable to return to Poland. I accepted.

After a long journey from north to south we arrived at a small station in the evening and took a taxi. There was a smell in the back of pickled onions. I could see hedge-rows and fields outside the car windows. We bumped down a lane and pulled up at what was to be our holiday home. It was a long low building with a tin roof and walls which were shedding their whitewash. We all went to bed. My room was at the end of the house. I lay awake looking out of the window. The moon stood low in the sky. It was large and white with grey shadings. Because of the moonlight the barks of the trees round about looked as if they had been brushed with silver and the grass was strangely luminous. I felt happy.

The days that followed, weather permitting, we spent down in the cove, a small inlet with a narrow spit of sand. At one end there were two squarish oblong rocks, one on top of the other, which formed a natural bench. While Mr Longhorn and 'the boys', as his twins were known, used to potter about with their shrimp nets, his wife Janice and I would sit there. She would knit – she was always knitting something to save money – and I would read or stare at the horizon.

Some feet below the bench, the rocks dropped in a set of natural steps or plates to the sea, the last being about a foot above the tide. When the sea rushed in, it climbed over the bottom lip, rushed to the next, climbed over that and continued upwards for as far as its strength would carry it. I started the holiday thinking of the sea as volatile, tempestuous, like human nature; sometimes calm and other times angry. But sitting on the bench beside Janice, her knitting needles clacking, I began to change.

'Have you ever thought of the sea as being like rubber?' I said to her one day.

She stopped knitting and looked downwards.

'It hadn't occurred to me before,' she replied, 'but you're quite right. It really does look as though it's moulding itself to the rocks.'

Together we stared at the water with its head of white foam rushing backwards and forwards. For the first time since I had come to England I had formulated an independent thought which could be considered by others and agreed upon. It was from that moment that I date my assimilation into the culture.

In 1942 I was an RAF fitter in North Africa. One evening a sergeant came to the barracks and I was told to report to the airfield immediately. When I arrived there was a transport plane standing on the runway with a lorry nearby. An officer told me that I was to take out the boxes that were in the back of the lorry and put them in the hold of the aeroplane. There were several other RAF personnel

there as well; cooks, cleaners, clerks and medical order-
lies, and together we set to.

Each of the boxes was about the size of the kind of box
that a croquet kit comes in. There were a great number
of them, probably several hundred in all, stacked under
the khaki awning of the lorry. When we came to lift them
we found they were extremely heavy and needed two
men to carry them. The work was exhausting and I was
soon sweating. As it began to grow dark, the two men in
front of me stumbled and dropped their box. It hit the
runway on one of its corners and split open. A moment
later there was a pile of coins glimmering on the tarmac.
The box had been filled with money. Everyone 'ummed'
and 'aahed' with amazement.

'You stupid fools,' shouted the officer.

Looking very foolish, the two men who had dropped
the box crouched down and began trying to gather up the
money.

'Get away from them,' bellowed the officer, 'and get
back to what you were doing. And you!'

I realised the officer was addressing me.

'. . . yes, you. Get a sandbag and clear them up.'

I found a sandbag behind an anti-aircraft gun. I ran
back to the pile of money, pushed aside the pieces of box,
and began to gather up the coins. Chink, chink, chink,
they sounded as they fell into the depths of the sack. I
was curious to know what denomination they were, but
it was too dark to see.

'Get a move on,' shouted the officer.

I redoubled my efforts.

When the bag was full, I twisted the top and lifted it
with great difficulty to the hands stretching down from
the hold of the aeroplane. Then I went back to where the
sections of shattered box lay, gathered them up and put
them at the side of the runway.

The job was finished. We lined up in rows.

'Slemic, stay behind,' shouted the officer. 'Everyone
else, dismiss.'

While the men slouched off down the runway, the
officer made me turn out all my pockets and take off my
boots and socks, in case I had stolen any of the money.
Naturally he found nothing.

118

'I'm sorry I had to ask you to do that,' he apologized. I was sitting on the running board of the lorry pulling my boots back on again. 'But I had to,' he continued. 'You understand, don't you?'

'Where's it going?' I asked, nodding towards the aeroplane. A man in overalls was pulling the chocks away from the wheels.

'Yugoslavia,' the officer said.

The next morning I got up before breakfast and went back to the airfield. There were small red flowers and blades of coarse grass growing in the sandy earth. Tyre marks from the transport plane stretched along the concrete like serpents. I found the pieces of box just where I had left them, and underneath the single coin I had managed to hide for myself. It was a sovereign, one of tens of thousands which I didn't doubt had filled all the boxes. I don't remember the year but it had a picture of George VI on it. I lost it later on leave in Cairo, in the back of a taxi.

I first met Eunice in 1950 outside the Strand Theatre. I had gone there to see a play and she was waiting outside for a date who never showed up. We started talking. I too was waiting for a friend. I asked her to join us. Afterwards, we all went and had a drink together in a pub. I asked Eunice if she was sad because the man she had been meeting had not shown up? Not a bit of it, she told us. If he had, she wouldn't have met us. Her philosophy was that every cloud had its silver lining. At the end of the evening she invited us to her twentieth birthday party. 'I expect a very big present,' she added. 'I love presents and I'm not at all ashamed to receive them.' Then she went off to stay with a relative in Great Portland Street as it was too far for her to go home that night.

The following weekend I caught the train alone (my friend couldn't come) to Seer Green in Buckinghamshire and found my way to Eunice's house. It stood in a road of red-brick villas and was itself large and ugly. The door was opened by Eunice's father. I looked at him and he seemed familiar. Then I recognised who he was. He had been the officer who had supervised the loading of the boxes of money onto the aeroplane. His handshake was vice-like.

'I think we've met before,' I said. I reminded him of the airfield in the desert. He said that he remembered me, but it might have been out of politeness. The doorbell rang again. I moved towards the hall.

'Through the door straight ahead, drinks on the left,' Eunice's father called after me. 'You'll find Eunice in there somewhere. Cloakroom at the bottom of the stairs. Very nice to meet you Mr Slemic.'

I went into the room to which he had pointed. Several couples were dancing around a record player at one end. The ceiling was decorated with Chinese lanterns and bunting, and there were sweet-smelling hyacinths growing in bowls on the sideboard. Large French windows looked into a garden filled with daffodils waving in the breeze. I didn't know a soul. I went over to the table in the corner and was given a glass of red drink by a middle-aged woman. 'Not very interesting, I'm afraid,' she apologised. I was nearly thirty and clearly much too old for non-alcoholic punch.

'You are?' she enquired.

'I'm August Slemic.'

'And I'm Eunice's mother, Heather Thomas, how do you do. Now she said I was to look out for you because you wouldn't know anyone, and to call her when you came. Eunice. Eunice? I understand you're Polish.'

'That's correct.'

'You speak very good English. Eunice, your friend is here.'

Eunice came over.

'How very good that you came, you Polish knight in shining armour,' she said.

'It's made of tin, my armour.'

I handed her my present, a large bunch of daffodils which I had bought at Marylebone station. I was a poorly paid junior in a City surveyor's and they were all I could afford.

'Not very imaginative,' I apologised.

I pointed at the cream-coloured heads swaying all round the lawn outside.

'It was awful of me to have demanded a present,' she said. 'Forgive-*moi*?'

We smiled at one another and I saw that she was really beautiful. Her blonde hair was cut short – almost like a bob – quite unlike the style of the times, and curved in just above the neck. Her eyes were midway between blue and grey and her face was wide, almost Slavic. She had a mole on the left side of her mouth above her chin which she had painted black. Her expression was wide and open.

'Many happy returns,' I said. I laid my hands on her shoulders and brought my lips to her cheeks.

'What are you drinking?' she asked.

I held up my glass.

'Oh no, not that concoction,' she said. 'Mother, you didn't give it to him. Not after what I told you. I don't believe it. It's for schoolboys. This is a war hero.'

'That might be putting it a little too high,' I said, and a few moments later accepted a large tumbler of diluted whisky from Mrs Thomas.

I was introduced to various young men who had all been or were in the Services because it was thought we would have something in common. The conversations which I had were boring and throughout them I kept searching for the slim, slight figure of Eunice in her blue silk dress. The lunch was a buffet and she came and sat beside me. Afterwards we pulled the curtains and all the guests played 'Murder in the Dark' although it wasn't very dark. When I drew the Ace of Spades, which was the murderer's card, I followed Eunice behind the piano and began to strangle her delicately.

'Oh no, I am dying, struck down in the bloom of my youth,' she cried theatrically and slid to the ground.

The woman screamed. The men shouted. The door was flung open and Mr Thomas who was the detective appeared with a torch which he shone around the room. During the interrogation I could not stop myself thinking that I had touched Eunice on her slim beautiful neck. Nor could I stop myself glancing at the body. Though I parried Mr Thomas' questions well (I knew how to hide behind my accent), this gave me away. Or it appeared to.

'Just as the criminal cannot stop himself from returning

to the scene of his crime, so the murderer cannot stop himself gazing at the corpse,' he said. 'Therefore, Mr Slemic, I accuse you of the murder of my daughter.'

I smiled and said that yes, it was me, and everyone applauded and said what a clever fellow Major Thomas was and how lucky his bank were to have him.

The curtains were pulled back: the French windows were thrown open to let in some air and it was time for tea. I went out to the large, cream-coloured utility kitchen to help.

'You were a very good murderer,' said Eunice as she took the damp cloths off the ready-made plates of sandwiches.

'Apparently not that good.'

'I'm sure you'd have got away with it if someone hadn't signalled your identity to father.'

'I think I gave it away myself without anyone else having a hand in it. I did keep looking at the corpse.'

'I quite agree with Eunice,' said Mrs Thomas. 'I love my husband dearly but I don't believe he could have worked it out on his own unless someone helped him. I think I know who's responsible but I'm not going to tell.'

I was mystified. Obviously more had been happening than I had been aware of.

Eunice went into the larder and a moment later came the sound of her humming beyond the door.

'I'm so pleased you could come today,' said Mrs Thomas. She was pouring milk out into little jugs. 'I wanted to thank you for looking after Eunice the other night and I wanted to say that I hope we'll see you again.'

I nodded.

'I'm sure you'll feel at home here,' she went on. 'We're not exactly English, you know. I have a French grandmother, on my mother's side. And there's also some Italian and maybe a bit of Russian.'

'Don't believe a word mother says.' It was Eunice coming back out of the larder with several butter dishes. 'We're just bog-Irish and Scotch, mongrels of the worst type. . . .'

By the time I caught my train that evening, I was in love with Eunice. My feelings were reciprocated. We started to see one another. We went to the theatre a great deal.

Eunice had aspirations to be an actress. She was a member of an amateur group and I used to help her with her lines. I started visiting her at her home on Sundays and later staying for weekends. I became friendly with her mother and father. He was dry and slow, but Heather Thomas I liked. She taught me how to play cribbage and when I had mastered the game presented me with a cribbage scoring board with ivory pegs. The board had been made by prisoners of war with whom she had worked. During the time of which I am speaking she was a prison visitor and much devoted to 'her men'. She vaguely disapproved of her daughter's interest in acting and continuously emphasised to Eunice the importance of getting her secretarial qualifications. Eunice was working for a small company manufacturing sanitary ware based in the western outskirts of London and attending a technical college part-time. I think the parents looked to me to put Eunice on what they called 'the straight and narrow'. I was happy to let them think this, but in fact nothing could have been further from my mind. I loved Eunice precisely because of her interest in the theatre, her gaiety and her laughter, which were all far away from the straight and narrow. I was serious and solid and hard-working but she was a free spirit and when I was with her, at least temporarily, I was set free myself. And then of course there was sex. One evening after we had been to the theatre I suggested that she came home with me.

'I thought you'd never ask,' she teased.

She telephoned her relative in Great Portland Street.

'No I'm not coming. *Triste*? Yes. I'm staying which a girl-friend,' she exclaimed. 'Oh yes, I shall be quite all right. She lives above a family of dwarfs and apparently they're very protective of young girls. They think we're all Snow White. Which of course we all are. Pure as the driven snow.'

Here she winked at me.

'Bye-bye.'

We left the telephone box and began to walk along the pavement.

'Wasn't I great?' she said.

'You were.'

We caught the bus to Holborn where I had a small

123

service flat. She wouldn't let me turn on any of the lights. Even the one in the hall. 'Darkness is so much more romantic,' she said. We undressed in my bedroom with our backs to one another and climbed into my narrow bed.

'Pooh! When did you last change your pillow-case? It smells of Brylcreem,' were her first words as she settled between the sheets.

'Last week.'

She put her arms around me. 'I love thee little August,' she said.

'And I like you too. I mean, I love you too.'

'How much?'

'About a ton's worth.'

'Is that all?'

'Ten ton's worth,' I said.

'Better.'

We made love with the buses outside rumbling towards Islington. I would not say it was a great success but it was not a fiasco either.

After this we became lovers and Eunice would often stay with the girlfriend who lived above the dwarfs. This went on for perhaps two years. During this time she never once asked if I was going to marry her. She simply assumed that I would because I was older and therefore reliable. Trust like this is the sincerest form of flattery.

We married in nineteen fifty-four and went to Ireland for our honeymoon, lured by tales of meat for dinner every day and twice on Sundays. In those days life in England was still extremely austere. We stayed in the Old Grounds Hotel in Ennis and spent our days sitting in bars or in bed making love, just as those who are newly married are meant to. Since the first time we had grown skilled and practised and we knew just how to touch and hold one another. Our passion was great, especially at night when we were always a little drunk, but strangely, what I remember of our love-making were those gentle times in the mornings: running my hands under her and pulling her deeper onto me; smelling the overpowering smell of her skin and hair and the brassy smell of her earrings; shivering from the feel of her hand cupping my testicles; hearing her whisper, '. . . I love you, I love you

124

. . .'; and suddenly the miracle beginning to happen like two drops of water on a window pane running into each other, and then tiredness and absolute peace. . . .

I first came to the street where we now live in nineteen fifty-six. As soon as I saw it I knew that I wanted to live here. Something about the trees along the pavement, the high walls around the gardens, the shapes of the houses, brought me straight back to Sunday afternoons in my childhood and to my uncle's villa outside the city. Slemic and Co. was two years old then. I bought our house the same year with the first flush of money I made.

In the beginning Eunice and I used to sleep in the same bed. This went on for some years, ten perhaps. Then we changed to separate beds but carried on sleeping in the same room. After Damian left to go to university, Eunice moved to the room next door leaving a spare bed in mine. My snoring and the way I talked at night was keeping her awake, she said.

When the separate sleeping arrangements were first introduced I was embarrassed. I did not want anyone to know that we did not sleep together. Consequently, on those days when Mavis the cleaning lady used to come, I would make the spare bed look as though it had been used. I hoped by this to make her assume that intimacy had taken place and that afterwards my wife had gone back to her room. This ploy went on for some time until one day I found myself at home when Mavis was around. I don't remember why. She was changing the sheets on my bed. As she did this I thought I'd better make my subterfuge convincing. 'Are you going to change the sheets on the other bed, Mavis?' I asked innocently. Mavis straightened up. She was a big woman; she still is. She has big arms like rolling pins. Her skin is very white and if she presses it, it retains the impression of her fingers for a moment or two. 'Change the sheets, Mr Slemic?' she said. 'Oh I don't think there's any need for that. That bed hasn't been slept in for months. It just gets ruffled up with you lying on it and reading. Mrs Slemic says you only read on it when you can't sleep, so she said there's no need to do it.' She tucked in the sheet on the far side of my bed. I stood still for a moment and then said, 'Yes of course, Mavis, you're quite right. There's no point in doing things if there's no need to do them.' I fled to the garden like someone who had been caught doing something wrong. So Eunice knew what I had been doing. She had not said anything about it to me, yet she had said something to Mavis. After that I never ruffled the bed again.

Like everything I got used to sleeping apart in the end. Then one Christmas we went away together. We ordered two separate rooms but what we got was a room with a double bed. We complained but the hotel was full. We had to take the room. It was a nightmare. Every night we were unable to sleep. Every night we tossed and turned. Every night we had to get out of bed several times to adjust our tangled nightwear. Where our bodies touched our skins heated up and roasted. It was like being a child again and having a fever. We quarrelled and blamed each other for everything. We drank great quantities of water. When we came back from Christmas we were exhausted. We slept for days. On New Year's Eve we were still tired. Our son invited us to his flat. But we wouldn't go. We stayed home, drank half a bottle of Lanson champagne together at midnight and then went to our respective beds.

On the evening I am recalling, Damian arrived around six as usual. He had just given up his university course – something I disapproved of – and was living in the flat of a friend in Battersea. We all had a couple of drinks and then he told us this story:

His friend in Battersea had chained his bicycle to the railings outside the flat. One evening the friend thought he heard a noise. He went outside and found a black youth trying to steal his bicycle. The friend got hold of the black and dragged him inside, intent on calling the police. At first the black protested his innocence but by the time he had been manhandled through the front door of the flat he realised he was in serious trouble.

'All right,' the black said, 'I did it. But if you call the police they're going to give me a hard time.'

At this point in the story Damian looked at Eunice and myself as if to say, 'Don't you see?'

'These black bastards,' continued Damian, 'they think they can come over here, break the law, and then expect to be let off because the police won't treat them kindly: "Please don't call the police – they'll hurt me." I ask you, it's bloody ridiculous. Why should there be one law for them and another for us?'

Damian's tone and line of argument infuriated me. I started to defend the youth.

After twenty minutes of argument Damian announced that he had to go. Furious, I followed him out to the steps to say goodbye. Coming back into the house, I slammed the front door angrily.

'Don't do that, it's just been re-painted,' Eunice shouted from inside.

I was angry with Eunice too. She had not said anything during the argument. Now, when I heard her, I decided that she had actually sided with her son.

That's it! I said to myself.

I re-opened the front door, went back outside and slammed it with all my might. (I later learnt it made some of the plates fall off the dresser in the kitchen.)

That will teach her! I told myself. Then, without stopping to think where I was going, I marched through the gate and away up the street.

A few minutes later I found myself in the local high street. It was summer-time. A bus lurched out of the Stamford Brook depot, honked its horn at a uniformed inspector and drove away towards Hammersmith. A woman stood outside the Kentucky Fried Chicken take-away, clipping and un-clipping her handbag.

I crossed the road and wandered towards where the shops are concentrated. Two men sat outside a public house in their shirt sleeves under a dusty umbrella. Their forearms were covered with a fine hair the same colour as the beer they were drinking. It was the quiet time between the end of work and the beginning of the evening.

Feeling dazed, almost intoxicated from my rage. I

meandered on. Buildings and people slipped by and I realised I did not know what I was going to do with myself. I noticed a neon sign flickering intermittently and read the words 'Star of India'. Marooned in the middle of the plate glass window below was a sign bearing the magic word 'Open'.

Why not? I thought.

I pushed on the corroded metal door frame. Inside it was dark and empty like a church. I noticed the sweet smell of old incense and, more faintly, something damp like rotting carpet.

I went towards a table in the far corner. It was underneath a huge fish tank filled with pebbles that reminded me of old sweets. There was a ragged length of hose at the side of the tank from which mercury-coloured bubbles were pouring out.

I sank onto a red velvet-covered chair and swivelled myself around. The table cloth where it hung down was a stiff screen which my legs had to push against.

I moved my side plate so that I could rest my elbows on the table. On the cloth underneath there were brown blotches.

I picked up the red bound folder marked 'Menu'. The dishes were listed behind a grubby plastic film.

My eyes wandered over the pages. But instead of retaining what I had read and making a choice, I found myself remembering the moment when I had slammed the front door and then trying to imagine Eunice's expression in the moments immediately after.

A waiter came to take my order. He wore a white coat with buttons. His skin had a sheen to it like a polished apple and he smelt of aftershave.

I ordered an onion baji with lime sauce, two spicy puppadums, prawn biryani, ladies' fingers, a nan and dhall, with a pint of lager to drink.

When the waiter had finished writing down the order, he put his biro away. On the part of his jacket just above the pocket there were dozens of pale blue biro lines and smudges. I was reminded of hanging tendrils of seaweed.

'Coming up sir,' he said and marched off.

A moment later the sound of voices began to drift from

the kitchen, followed by the clatter of a saucepan being lifted onto a stove.

I settled back in my chair. The anger which had carried me there was still circulating in my system. I told myself that I had been brave to do what I had done. By leaving the house, instead of going back into the room and arguing until Eunice and I were hoarse, I had managed to break with a previously cast-iron pattern of behaviour. It would teach Eunice a lesson and one day I would teach Damian as well. . . .

I lifted the pint of lager which the waiter had brought and took a gulp. It was fizzy and without taste. I immediately associated it with the bubbles fizzling in the fish tank.

I began to turn the ice-cold lager glass round and round. A circle of wet from the condensation formed on the white cloth. I could not stop myself wondering if Eunice was all right and, a moment later, I became aware of a sort of tugging ache at the thought of her in pain.

I moved the glass and began to form another circle beside the first, thus making a figure of eight. I was determined not to succumb to these morbid thoughts.

I looked up from the tablecloth and took another drink. The wallpaper was yellow with red figures in velvet standing in relief. The figures were a man and a woman in Regency dress: she in a long gown and bonnet, he in a buttoned swallowtail coat and breeches. The woman had one foot on the step of a coach and the man was assisting her.

'Just a few more minutes and we'll be ready, sir.'

I looked up. It was the waiter calling to me from behind the bar. He was smiling broadly and his teeth showed white between his lips.

'Thank you,' I replied.

There was a clunking noise and the sound of sitar and tabla music began to crackle from a loudspeaker.

I turned towards the fish tank. The ache had returned. I stared gloomily into the water. It was lit up by a neon strip sellotaped to the top. The ends of the tank were painted blue like a swimming pool. I looked at the fish. Some were long and thin, their bodies like cigar cylinders. Others were flat with long white tendrils which waved like pieces of underwater weed. Others again were the colour of truffles, and had long black dangerous-looking whiskers on either side of their mouths. Their proper names in Latin were given in labels stuck into the pebbles, just like the labels in potted plants. I tried to read one of them but could not concentrate for the ache.

I sank back into my chair and looked out of the window. Because of the net curtains I could only see the top parts of houses on the other side of the street. They were red brick Victorian. I saw a woman pass across a window drinking from a can. All over I imagined men and women were in their rooms alone. The men were clipping their nails or putting cartons of milk into old refrigerators that smelt vaguely of gas. The women were looking through glossy magazines or shaving under their arms. If I could focus on these ideas hard enough, I hoped I would be able to block out the painful images of Eunice in distress, which were pressing on my thoughts. . . .

Two heated dishes with candles burning underneath were set down in front of me. The meal followed. Watching the waiter set down the stainless steel dishes, once again I told myself that I was hungry.

'Enjoy your meal,' said the waiter, pointing with his hand. His palm, which was uppermost, was pink with strong dark lines running across it. It was not dark like his skin as I had expected.

'Thank you,' I said.

'More lager?' He waved towards the three-quarters empty glass.

'No thank you,' I replied.

The waiter left me. I broke off a piece of nan. It was hot and I felt grease on my finger tips. I dipped the bread into the dhall and saw it was greyish and watery like gruel.

I lifted the bread into my mouth and began to chew. The food was almost without flavour. I noticed the sitar and tabla music had given way to modern pop.

I swallowed. The dhall left a faint aftertaste like sour milk.

You will enjoy yourself! I repeated inwardly. I heaped prawn biryani onto the plate with a heavy spoon which was embossed with the name of a hotel in Manchester.

The rice was yellow; the prawns had a slight inky-blue tinge to them; and the sauce reminded me of diluted peanut butter. I put some onto my fork and transferred it to my mouth. Suddenly I didn't feel in the least hungry. I began to chew. The rice was hard like uncooked pasta and the prawns were stringy. I swallowed and immediately felt nauseous.

I put down the heavy knife and fork and looked once again out of the window. The houses on the other side of the street were a blur. In my mind's eye I saw Eunice sitting in our front room trying to watch televison but listening for the sound of my key in the front door. Or standing by the gate, staring anxiously down the street. Or lying on her bed crying, with her eyes puffed up and her hair stuck to her wet face.

I flattened out the food on my plate hoping to give the impression that there was less there than there actually was.

'Excuse me,' I called out, 'could I possibly have my bill, please?'

The waiter was behind the bar. He put down the copy of the newspaper which he was reading and walked over, clicking his pen as he came.

'You did not like your meal?' he asked brusquely, seeing the almost untouched food.

'No, I do like it, it's very good,' I replied. 'It's just that, when I came in, I felt hungry but now I don't feel hungry any more. I don't know what it is. Perhaps it's a bug. . . .'

I touched my stomach, hoping the gesture would make my reply more plausible.

'You want anything else?' the waiter persisted.

'No thank you . . . honestly . . . I'm not hungry.'

'You want tea or coffee?'

'No, thank you, I don't want anything,' I replied. 'I just want the bill.'

The waiter went back to the bar, climbed onto a stool and began to write it out.

I tapped my foot and gazed towards the door. My eye was caught by a large, plastic reproduction of Kali. She wore a funny shaped hat; her eyes were staring; and on one of her arms someone had hung 'The Star of India Take Away Menu and Prices'.

* * *

131

I ran up the steps to our front door with my key in my hand and stopped. I hoped to hear the sound of the television droning in the living room. But no sound came from within.

I inserted the key and turned the latch. The door opened and I stepped onto the doormat.

'Eunice?' I called.

The house was silent.

'Eunice?' I called again.

I slammed the door and went into the hall.

'Eunice?' I said more quietly. There was a slight noise in the front room. It was a settling sound, like someone moving on a couch. It flashed across my mind that there might be someone else in the house with me besides Eunice.

'Is that you in there, Eunice?' I called out.

My heart began to beat hard.

I stood absolutely still in the hall, straining my ears to hear what was happening. Then suddenly I saw that there was someone else in the hall besides myself. It was a dark figure standing beside and behind me to my left.

The speed at which my heart was beating increased. Clearly and insistently I told myself to find something to throw at the intruder.

At the bottom of the stairs there was a table with a table weight sitting on it. It was four steps away, I calculated. That was a long way to go and, for all I knew, the man behind me could probably move faster than I could. I looked to the left and the right, hoping to see something else but there was nothing.

There was no alternative. I had to turn and face whoever it was.

I started to turn. Simultaneously the figure started to turn. My heart raced. I poised myself to shout or strike out. . . .

It was with shock a fraction of a second later that I recognised the familiar outline of the coconut-shaped head.

The intruder had been my own reflection, seen out of the corner of my eye in the full-length mirror.

My heart was still beating hard, pushing against my ribs, and I could feel my knees were trembling. I dimly thought that it was the sort of situation that should make one laugh but I did not feel like laughing.

From the living room came the noise which I had heard before. I ran forward and looked in. At first I thought that it was empty. Then I saw that it was not.

'Eunice?' I said.

She was lying on her front on the sofa. Her face was buried in her hands and her blonde hair was spread out on the cushions.

'Are you all right? Are you asleep?'

Eunice did not respond but lay there absolutely still.

I went across to the sofa and sat down on the edge.

'Eunice?'

I took her shoulders. They were warm. I shook her gently.

'Are you asleep?'

She moved her head ever so slightly as if grinding it into the sofa.

I bent forward and kissed the back of her head. Her hair was fine and smelt of shampoo and other, less distinguishable smells.

'Eunice . . . I'm sorry. . . .'

'Come on, darling. Turn round to me.'

She moved again.

'Come on, sweetie. . . .'

I took her shoulders and tried to roll her over. Her body was heavy and unyielding. Suddenly she turned, threw her arms around my waist and lifted her head onto my lap.

'I'm so sorry, my darling,' I said, 'for what I did. . . .'

I tried to turn her face so that I could look at her, but she would not let me. With my fingers I felt that her skin was wet and that matted strands of her hair were stuck to it.

I bent forward and brought my mouth close to her ear.

'Talk to me, say something,' I whispered.

'Do you love me?' she asked falteringly.

'Of course I do,' I said.

'You won't go off like you did this evening, ever again, will you? It was only a silly argument about a bicycle.'

'No, of course I won't,' I promised.

'I love you,' she said.

She lifted herself up and put her arms around my neck. A moment later I felt her moist cheek against mine.

'My little mongoose,' she whispered.

'My dear one. I'm so sorry for what I did.'

'I was so worried,' she continued, 'when you went out. First I went and stood in the street, but you didn't appear. Then I came back in here and started trying to watch television but I couldn't. Then I began to think you were never coming back and I started crying.'

I drew back from Eunice and began to pick away the wet strands of hair which were stuck to her face. The tip of her nose was red and around her eyes her mascara had run and trickled like ink into the tiny fissures that were everywhere in her skin.

'I won't do it again, I promise,' I said.

'You really promise?'

She stared at me with her pale blue eyes. The whites around them were bloodshot. Her expression was a childish mixture of yearning and wary watchfulness. It pleaded for love and, at the same time, it appeared to be waiting for the tiniest hint that promises would be broken. From past experience I knew that if I gave her the slightest opportunity to doubt me, she would do so with a vengeance and we would end up shouting at each other all night.

I smiled at her and pinned her hair behind her ears.

'Those are nice earrings,' I said.

They were long and golden.

'They're the new look,' she said.

We put our arms around one another and began to rock gently backwards and forwards.

Outside the long windows night began to fall. The elm tree became a dark, indistinct shape. The lights came on downstairs in the house opposite and the street lamps began to cast their yellow light.

Eunice separated herself from me. I saw her familiar profile, her long nose, her neatly cut hair running in a straight line along the bottom of her neck.

'Can I ask you something?' she asked.

'Of course,' I said blithely.

'Did you have an Indian?' She spoke in her friendliest voice and poked me on my knee.

134

'Yes,' I said.

I covered my mouth with my hand. I could not see her expression but I could imagine that she was smiling.

'It was ghastly,' I added, mumbling through my fingers. 'I couldn't eat a thing.'

She started to laugh and after a moment or two I began to laugh with her.

1981:
Night

We drove past the dark spire of the War Memorial and into the upper reaches of Wimbledon.

'My first girlfriend lived near here,' I said.

'Oh.'

'She was called Mary. She worked in one of the big houses on the common. I used to come over from Richmond where I lived to see her.'

Outside a restaurant a cluster of people stood on the pavement. The women were all holding handbags and where their skin was bare it seemed more than usually pale. Laughter drifted through my window and an aroma of food. The driver in front discarded a cigarette which exploded on the road. There was a melancholy about the close of this summer's evening and everyone going home.

'Did you go for walks with her on Wimbledon Common?' I heard Marjorie asking.

'To tell you the truth, I don't remember much about her at all,' I replied.

'You fickle men. You love us and leave us and you don't remember the details.'

'What makes you say that?' I asked.

'Oh it's a long story,' she said.

In front of us a belisha beacon winked, a woman with a poodle standing below it.

I stopped and waved the woman over.

'But you are a gentleman,' Marjorie said, 'I'll give you that.'

I suddenly felt that something was touching me on the back of my neck. It took me a moment to realize what it was. Marjorie was stroking me.

139

'I like gentlemen,' she said.

I drove round the corner and saw we were at the top of Wimbledon Hill. The blue-coloured tarmac of the road dipped away and levelled out below. There were trees on either side with apartment blocks behind them.

'Sometimes, on a clear day, you can see the Downs. Or at least so I'm told,' she said.

In the foreground I could see yellow street lamps and the shapes of buildings whilst further away the architecture merged into the darkness and the street lamps became smaller and smaller points of light. Suddenly I was filled with a sense of all the thousands of people in these distant suburbs in front of me, who were living their lives at that very moment. Were their actions mysteriously balanced? I wondered. For a bad deed done here, a good deed done there? I was beginning to regret that I had come.

'Have the stars begun to shine?' I asked.

We were drawing towards the bottom.

'Yes,' she said. 'There's a bit of a moon too.'

We passed Ely's department store with mannequins in bright swim-suits in several of the windows, and the forecourt of the railway station with three taxis drawn up, their yellow 'For Hire' signs showing.

Two miles further on Marjorie said, 'Turn left there,' and pressed my neck. 'Then take the next right.'

I turned into the street.

There were cars parked on either side with low ugly houses behind.

We turned again. I stared intently ahead. The tarmac was a reddish hue.

I was trying to decide what I would do when Marjorie asked me in. If I said no to her invitation it would seem sullen. But if I agreed, what would it lead to? The obvious answer was to say yes, for half an hour, but when has that ever worked? Then I started thinking about Eunice. It was past midnight and she would soon be going to bed. She always went to bed when I was out and she went without the slightest qualms. I was suddenly grateful that Eunice and I had at least achieved that much.

Suddenly, some way down the road, I saw the outline of a cat lit up by the head-lamps of an oncoming car. Marjorie let out a noise halfway between a gasp and a scream. The cat looked as though it was suspended in the air and I realised it was about to be hit. My foot found the brake and my left arm went across to prevent Marjorie jolting forward as I stopped. This all happened before I could think.

We pulled over and got out. The oncoming car, a Ford Cortina, had stopped in the middle of the road with its lights winking. As we hurried past, I saw there were young faces inside staring out at us through the windows.

The cat was lying behind on the road, its position was the same as when it had seemed suspended. Its coat was black with a white underbelly and it had white paws. A dark smear of blood matted the hair around the face. The animal was dead.

I heard the sound of a door opening and tinny music. We turned round. One of the back doors of the Cortina had swung open and a blonde girl had put her head out.

'What was it?' she asked gently.

From behind someone pushed the girl and she tumbled inelegantly onto the tarmac to the sound of riotous laughter.

'You lot had better start behaving or you're going to get thick ears,' the girl shouted through the open door.

She got back to her feet and dusted the side of her white skirt.

'What was it?' she asked again.

'It was a cat,' said Marjorie.

'I'm so sorry. It wasn't yours, was it?'

'No,' said Marjorie, shaking her head.

The girl came up and looked at the dark shape lying on the road. I noticed a lolly stick beside it.

'Poor thing,' she said.

A dark head poked out of the driver's window and said, 'Sorry about that. It must have got dazzled by the headlamps.'

'I'm so glad it wasn't your pet but I'm still sorry,' said the girl.

Holding her necklace between her teeth, the girl went back to the car and climbed in. The door shut. Again the pale young faces stared from inside. Their expressions were exactly the same as I had seen at fires and at motorway accidents.

Their car cruised away. I watched its lights growing smaller and smaller and heard the tinkling cassette player fading. It was like a ship moving on a dark sea. I was overcome by a great feeling of sadness.

At the far corner the car turned and we were left in silence.

I looked up and down the street. Nothing was moving. I heard Marjorie knocking on a door. It was opened cautiously and Marjorie began to speak to the house-holder in low tones.

I touched the underside of the cat with the tip of my shoe. It was like a bag of water. Then I moved the lolly stick which was lying nearby away.

I let my eyes rest on the horizon where the night sky shaded to pale red. Far away, a train clattered along its tracks.

'Here,' said Marjorie.

I took the two pieces of cardboard which she was holding. She shook out a black plastic bag and turned on the borrowed torch.

I crouched down. The narrow beam lit up the animal's fur. There was blood trickling from the mouth. The neck was long and limp.

I began to work the cardboard under the body. The difficulty of the manoeuvre said 'dead' to me more strongly than the blood or the lifelessness.

When I had done I rose slowly to my feet.

Marjorie pulled open the bag and shone the torch into it. It was like looking down into a well at night.

I dropped everything, the carcass and the cardboard. The body landed on its back, with the head twisted round to the side.

As Marjorie walked away I blew my nose. I heard a gate scraping open and, a moment later, low murmurs of gratitude.

I put my handkerchief back in my pocket, and remembered the party where we had been only a couple of hours before. Drinking the toast in the kitchen and later, standing in the garden. Marjorie telling me earnestly and drunkenly about her husband and her divorce whilst nearby, a woman sank into the grass in her high heels and collapsed, shrieking with laughter, *'Aide-moi, aide-moi. . . .'*

I had felt excited when Marjorie and I had left the party and walked up Hamilton Terrace under the trees towards my car. But now I felt a sort of numbness. I felt like a tortoise shrunk into its shell.

'Penny for your thoughts.'

Marjorie was beside me again.

'I was trying to remember the names of the stars,' I lied.

We started to walk. She linked my arm and rested her hand on mine.

'I hate to see anything die,' she said.

I heard my shoes and hers sounding on the road below us.

'You're married?'

'I told you I was,' I said.

'Does your wife have affairs?'

'If she did I wouldn't know.'

'What are you feeling now?'

'I'd like to think that whatever I do makes some small contribution to happiness,' I replied.

We had reached the car. She stepped past the bonnet and onto the pavement.

'Do you have affairs?' she asked.

She turned to look at me.

'No,' I said. 'Never.'

I opened the car door. As she got in I saw from her knees down to her ankles.

'Gentlemen aren't meant to look,' she said, 'but this time I'll make an exception.'

The hall of her flat was long and windowless. There was a mirror on one side covering the entire wall. The carpet was grey. If there had been a telephone kiosk it would have passed as a hotel lobby.

I followed after her through the front door. When the latch clicked I reminded myself I could leave any time I wished.

The first thing I noticed was an unmistakable feminine smell which I associated with nylons drying on towels and Ponds face cream. Through a door on my left, I glimpsed the white outline of a bath.

Marjorie undid the headscarf around her neck and laid it on a shelf in a cupboard inside. Her handbag came off her arm and went beside it.

I noticed a broomstick decorated with green tinsel and a black pointed hat with a brim, standing in a corner below.

'Halloween,' said Marjorie, catching my eyes. 'I'm really a secret witch.'

She shut the cupboard and stared into the mirror.

'Mirror, mirror on the wall, who's the fairest of them all?' she whispered hoarsely.

She squinted her eyes, lifted her chin and screwed up her mouth.

'Why, you are, Popeye,' she squawked.

'Very good,' I said.

'When I was a kiddie I wanted to go on the stage.'

Marjorie adjusted her headband and touched her hair.

'I'm thinking of getting it cut. What do you think?' she asked.

'I think it's nice long,' I replied.

'When you start a new life you have to change everything. I've changed my flat. I don't have a husband any more. I have a job. So maybe I should change my hair.'

I followed her to the living room. Four spotlights threw beams of light onto the white shag carpet. A glass-topped table stood in the corner with an empty bowl in the middle. Venetian blinds hung in front of the windows. A smell of new concrete and drying emulsion hung in the air.

'Sit. Sit.' She waved towards the cream-coloured three-piece suite and disappeared into the kitchen.

In the middle of the sofa there was a book lying open where I intended to put myself. Lifting it away, I saw that it was called *How to Live Your Own Life*.

'Would you like a coffee and a cognac?'

'Yes,' I said and sat down.

I leant back on the cushions. The sofa was too soft for comfort. I leant forward and looked around. On one wall there was a picture of a Coca-Cola bottle lid which appeared to be weeping, and on another hung a poster

144

of James Dean carrying a rifle. Marjorie banged away in the kitchen.

When I had finished examining the pictures, I turned my attention to the table in front of me which was strewn with magazines and books with bright covers. I picked up a handful and began to read the covers one by one: *How to Succeed at Sex, Calorie Countdown – Subtract to Slim, Perfect Woman, Super Woman, Life Begins at Forty*.

'Enjoying yourself?'

I looked up and saw Marjorie holding a tray. I hurriedly made a space.

'It's always very tempting in a strange house to peek and pry,' she said.

She put down the tray. The brown earthenware mugs were steaming. There was a smell of coffee.

'I remember one of the first times I went to see my husband in college,' she said. 'His room mate showed me into the sitting room and left me in there alone.'

Marjorie sat down on the sofa and crossed her legs.

'On the mantelpiece there were several postcards of Africa, and I knew he had a girlfriend who'd been out there. I desperately wanted to look at the backs of the cards to see if they were from her but at the same time I thought: What happens if he comes in? I had a good listen at the door to see if there was any activity outside and finally I plucked up enough courage to do it. Of course every one of the bloody cards was blank and I was holding one of the damn things when Peter marched in. "Caught in the act," he said. "Trying to see if there was anything written on the backs of my postcards." I said that post-cards were public and that anyone could look at them. And that's how we started our courtship I suppose. I'm not boring you, am I? Talking about my ex?'

She straightened herself up.

'Anyway, it's all water under the bridge now.'

I took the wine-glass filled with brandy which she was holding out to me.

'What do you think about him now?' I asked. 'If you don't mind my asking.'

'Oh Christ, I don't mind. Ask away. I don't have any secrets.' I could see her eyes darkening and the skin visibly tightening over her bones. 'What do I think about

145

him? Well, our marriage died a long time ago, and now it's buried and it's rotting in the ground,' she said. 'I don't think much about him. In fact. I don't think about him at all. I don't need him, thank you very much. I'm my own woman. Cheers.'

'Your health,' I replied.

The brandy both warmed and burnt as it went down my throat.

She dipped a sugar cube into her drink, staining it brown. 'Here. A treat for you for being such a good listener,' she said.

I opened my mouth and she put it on my tongue. 'In the name of the Father, the Son and the Holy Ghost,' she said in a mock priest-like voice.

I closed my lips. The cube disintegrated. The taste at the back of my throat was sweet.

'Good, isn't it?'

I nodded.

'My favourite. I could have them all day.'

A stained cube went into her own mouth.

'Mmmhh,' she exclaimed, smiling and chewing. 'The first time I had them was after a May Ball with Peter. We'd stayed up all night and in the very early morning we went in a punt up the river. He gave me his dinner jacket to keep me warm, and produced a small bottle of brandy and a packet of sugar cubes which for some reason he had in his pocket. We used the cap as a glass and watched the dawn coming. Mist rose off the banks and there were curlews piping amongst the needs. It was one of the happiest moments of my life.'

'Come here,' she said.

When I did not move she leaned forward and dabbed the side of my mouth with the moistened end of her forefinger.

'Sugar,' she said, showing me the granules stuck to the skin at the top. 'I'm sorry I keep talking about the past. I promise I won't do it any more.'

She brought the finger to her mouth and licked it.

'Your leg's shaking,' she said.

She was looking down. I looked in the same direction and saw that she was right. I was surprised, not only not to have noticed it but because inwardly I felt calm.

I felt Marjorie taking my hand and let her pull it towards her. I felt her rubbing it and then pressing it down on something soft. I turned my head slowly and saw that it was resting on her breast.

In my imagination I saw a grey landscape stretching to meet grey clouds on a distant horizon.

She was smiling at me and moving my hand gently downwards. Under the blouse I could feel the bumpy outline of her brassiere.

She uncrossed her legs. Her skirt dipped like a hammock. She lifted my hand and placed it in the space between her thighs.

I was aware of the swell of her stomach as it rose above her groin, the silky fabric of her spotted polka dot skirt, and more faintly, the bushiness of her pubic hair growing within the crease.

'I bet your wife doesn't understand you,' she said.

James Dean was looking down at me from the wall. I felt anxious about what I was going to do with my glass.

Marjorie had closed her eyes, parted her lips and was slowly leaning towards me.

I lay back on the pillow with my head resting on my hands. My clothes were folded tidily on a chair in front of the dressing table.

The room was small with cupboards on either side of the double bed. The patterned curtains over the windows hung down unevenly, having torn in places from their brass rings. The sheets when I had eased into them had been ever so slightly damp.

The lavatory flushed. Marjorie would soon be with me. My penis felt small and cold and my testicles had partially withdrawn into my body.

The door opened and she appeared in a pink dressing gown with white ruffs.

She turned off the overhead light and padded noise-lessly across the room.

I felt the mattress shifting as she settled on the edge of the bed.

She smiled at me and began to undo the cord around

147

her waist. I reached forward and took her arm. She sank towards me, her breasts falling free.

There was an intoxicating smell of face cream and shampoo.

Her nose brushed mine. It was cold. Our lips touched. I heard her gown falling on the floor, the sound just like snow when it slides from a branch.

The side light clicked off. I lifted back the duvet. I sensed her breasts touching my chest. Our tongues met. I felt that hers was wide and rounded at the end. I could taste her toothpaste.

She lay on her back. I found her belly button and let my finger slip into it. Her flesh was soft and ample.

I put my hand on her sex. The crease felt strangely dry as I rubbed my finger up and down.

I felt her fingers touching me, clumsily stroking my glans. She rose up from the pillow and motioned me to lie back. I heard a rustle of bedclothes and a moment later I was aware of her holding my penis in her mouth. She cupped my genitals with her hands and moved her head up and down. I thought I could feel her teeth touching my skin.

Her head came out from under the bed clothes.

'Just do it,' she said.

She lay back and lifted her knees. I put saliva on my fingers and reached down into the bed. When I found her sex I began to wet it gently. It felt warmer and moister than before.

I raised my body up and onto my elbows and lifted myself between her legs. She held my penis and pulled it into herself.

'Do it with all your might,' she urged.

I pressed with my hips and slid forward. Her sex was warm around mine.

A sudden picture of Eunice flashed across my thoughts, a memory from our early times together many years before. I saw her with her head resting on my thigh and my sex in her mouth. She was looking up at me and raising her eyebrows.

I could sense my excitement rising. I wanted to ask Marjorie to put her hand around my genitals but I knew there was not time.

148

The image of Eunice disappeared and I was filled with a new sensation; that of lying on Eunice and holding her and her holding me.

I was like a helium balloon that had just been let go and was gently rising from a noisy street into a quiet sky.

As my seed trickled out, Marjorie pulled my ear to her mouth.

'. . . oh baby . . . oh Peter . . .' she murmured.

We clung together in the darkness. I could not tell for how long. I had only one thought: that I should have been feeling something and I didn't know what it was.

My penis shrank and came out of her sex. I lifted myself away and lay back on the bed. I found a hand and entwined my fingers between hers.

'I'm sorry,' she said.

'Don't be sorry,' I heard myself saying. 'You've nothing to be sorry about. I'm the one who should say sorry.'

'I suppose we could say we're both out of practice.'

As I laughed I felt her convulsing beside me. I reached out and touched her face. It was hot with tears.

'Come here,' I said.

I put my arms around her and drew her to me.

'I haven't had a man, God, I don't know in how long.'

'Me neither. I mean I haven't been with a woman.'

'We're a pair of prize buffoons,' she said.

She started to cry and put her face against my neck. I felt my skin getting wet and stroked her back. In the pit of my stomach there was a small knot of pain. I felt it swelling up and then rising to the back of my throat. I wanted to cry but knew that I would not be able to and that the pain would stay like a bag of water pressing on the back of my face. I searched for words of comfort but the pain had pushed everything out of my mind. I doubled my strokes hoping that would make up for what I was not able to say.

'It's so good to be held,' murmured Marjorie, moving closer.

'We're just like animals. All we want is the warmth of another,' I said.

I was slipping from consciousness. I laid my arm across Marjorie's waist. She put her cold feet between my calves. I could feel the callouses on her little toes.

My head rolled to the side and I felt myself tumbling towards sleep.

New Year's Eve, December 31st 1980

At last I have my prisoner story, the one I was thinking about three days ago. I picture a prison with tall grim grey walls and a huge wooden gate that creaks on hinges. I picture the inside of the prison; the small wooden doors of the cells leading off gantries of metal which clang as the warders patrol up and down them. I picture the roof of glass that stretches above and lets light into the central well, wind whining in the gaps between the panes and water leaking through when there's a storm. I picture a cell, a small coffin-shaped oblong of stone, with a narrow barred window set high in the wall and a narrow wooden pallet for a bed. Now I picture the prisoner: a youngish man lying face to the wall with a grey blanket thrown over his shoulder. Through the tiny window he can hear momentous events going on in the streets around, for this prison stands in a city, not in the countryside. He can hear gunfire, the sound of breaking glass, and shouting voices. Darkness falls and some time in the middle of the night the prison gates are battered down. He hears the sound of running feet ringing on the metal gantries and cries of jubilation as the crowd who have battered down the gates run through the prison. Doors are unlocked and prisoners are set free. The prisoners whoop with delight as they step through their open cell doors.

My prisoner is the further cell in the most obscure part of the prison. His sentence is life imprisonment. As a cruel jest the authorities have had his cell constructed so that the lock is on the inside. Every time the door is to be unlocked the key has to be handed in through the Judas hole and he has to do it himself. The reason for putting the lock on the inside is so that the means to liberty is constantly before him, and also so that when he has to unlock the door himself a fleeting sense of what it would be to set himself free is momentarily his.

The prisoner hears the revolutionaries who are setting the other prisoners free getting closer and closer. At last they reach his door. His Judas hole is pushed open. A hand comes through clutching a large key. The key to his cell. The key is an old friend: he knows it well. It's a huge black key with string wrapped around the handle. The string is dirty with age and so worn the individual strands have merged into one.

'We found this outside your cell,' says a voice. 'Unlock your door and set yourself free.' The prisoner does not respond but goes on staring at his wall. 'Come on,' urges the voice. Still no response from the prisoner. The hand withdraws and an eye peers through the Judas hole. It is dark like an olive with possibly a scar underneath.

'Are you all right? Won't you take the key?' asks the one with the dark eye.

The prisoner raises his arm and waves it weakly. The gesture is unmistakable. No, he does not want the key. The speaker puts his arm in again and throws the key on the floor. The Judas hole bangs shut. Footfalls are heard receding. The key is on the floor. The prisoner continues to stare at the wall.

Out in the prison exercise yard fires are lit. The prison rum store is broken into and a party begins. All night long the prisoner hears voices, speeches, laughter. In the early morning the noises of merriment die away. Silence comes. For two days silence reigns supreme. For two days the prisoner lies exactly as the man who came to free him found him, not moving except to drink water from the tap in the corner of his cell. At the end of the two days there is a distant noise of trucks. A little later he hears the sound of marching feet and the sound of manacled legs dragging up the stairs. These are familiar sounds to him. He has heard them during his years of captivity. Now comes the sounds of cell doors banging open and shut. After two days of nothing happening, the prison is being used as a prison again. The victors are locking up the people who once locked them up.

152

That night the prisoner hears the familiar sound of the supper trolley clanking along the gantry towards him. A moment later he is by the Judas hole, waiting for the warder to rap on the wood. The rap comes, sweeter than anything he has ever known in his life up to that moment. With joy in his heart he puts his mess can on the ledge on his side of the Judas hole and knocks in return. The flap lifts up and the sweet familiar hand with 'Death' tattooed on the knuckles – it is the hand of the evening duty warder who served under the previous regime – comes through the hatch and removes the mess can. The warder has been re-employed, like all the old prison personnel, by the new powers. A moment later the prisoner's can comes back filled with thin vegetable soup, and along with it comes a piece of black bread. 'Slop out at ten o'clock,' says the warder outside.

The prisoner puts his bread under the mattress in the place which he calls his larder. He will eat it later. At the bedrock where he exists, every experience is savoured and every richness is wrung from it. He sits on the pallet and peers into the murky liquid in his can. Slivers of carrot and turnip lie on the bottom along with a single green bean. He will swallow the liquid first. Then the solids. And at the end he will have his favourite, the green bean. His heart is joyful. What happiness. Existence is returning to its previous pattern. He is beginning to feel safe again.

Now there is only one more detail to be taken care of. That night, shortly before slopping out, the prisoner throws the key onto the landing. The warder with the tattoo on his hand finds it, thinks nothing of it (after all, there has just been a revolution), and hangs it on the hook outside the door. At last everything is back to what it was.

Time passes. Prison life continues. The authorities assume the prisoner must have done something against them, for otherwise why else would he be in prison? So there is no chance he will be rooted out and expelled into the world. No. He will be left quite undisturbed by authority, except when it comes to give him his food, or to take away his slop bucket, or when it sends the barber, as it does once a week, to shave his beard, cut his finger-nails, and enquire after his health.

1981:
Morning

I woke up and felt for my wrist-watch under the pillow. It was five o'clock. Beyond the patterned curtains grey light glimmered and the birds had started their dawn chorus. I turned my head. Marjorie lay with the covers pulled over and the top sheet moved with her breath. Drifting towards sleep the night before, an idea had come to me through the pain. That I might wake up and not remember where I was, just like the adventurers in the books of my childhood. But I was not in the least surprised to wake up in a strange bed, and I remembered everything that had happened with absolute clarity. I lay still for a moment, staring at the crack that ran across the ceiling, and tried to consider how I felt. The pain no longer seemed to be pressing behind my face. My mood was suppressed but not anguished.

I slipped quietly out of bed, found my boxer shorts on the chair and pulled them on. Behind me Marjorie muttered something in her sleep. I turned to face her, trying to think what I would say if she woke up. I didn't really know myself. That I had to hurry home to Eunice? That it had all been a terrible mistake? That I was fleeing the unknown and hurrying back to what I knew? I waited, watching the dark top of her head on the pillow, expecting it at any moment to rise up and for her to open her eyes. But nothing happened. Her breathing became calm again. I took my clothes and shoes with one hand and my jacket with the other and crept out of the room, taking care to ensure that the keys in my pocket did not jangle.

In the bathroom I found a Bic ladies' razor lying inside a bath hat. I shaved with soap and lukewarm water. As the suds drained away I looked in the mirror. My skin was reddened and there was a small cut under my nose. I wiped away the spot of blood. In the sink my bristles lay like grey flecks of iron.

I went back to the living room to the glass-topped table where I had left my clothes. They were like figures on a mortuary table. After I had got dressed I looked for a pen beside the pile of self-help books but could not find one. Then I went into the kitchenette and found a Snoopy pad hanging from the cork message board with a Snoopy biro attached.

I pulled out a leather-backed chair and sat down at the glass table. Now that I had it in front of me I saw the pad was a 'Dream Record' where Snoopy lovers could write their dreams. I thought for a few seconds as I clicked the pen and began to write.

July 29th 1981

Dear Marjorie,

Today is the Royal Wedding. I hope you have a nice time watching it on television and painting your toenails as you said you were going to last night. I might watch some of it myself but I'm not a great one for television. I think I shall go for a walk in Holland Park: it's my favourite and it should be empty today.

Thank you for everything.

A

When I finished I read the note over. It was hard to connect the words on the paper, which were clearly in my own writing, with anything that I felt. It was as if they were written by a stranger. When I reached the end I thought about underlining 'Thank you for everything'. That would be something of me. I reached out with my pen. But in the end I decided it would give altogether the wrong impression.

I folded the paper in half, wrote 'Marjorie' on the front and stood it on the table like a menu. I was careful to select a position where she would see it when she came out of the bedroom. Now that it was done I did not really feel anxious any more. I wanted to leave, but not immediately. Yet I ought to go now if I were going. I stood up, took my keys from my pocket and turned towards the door. Halfway across the room my resolve crumbled. The funny thing is at the back of my mind, I had known what I was going to do all along.

I went into the kitchenette and banged the coffee pot on the stove. In one of the cupboards there were two large cups. I gave them a rinse because they looked dusty inside and put them on a tray. I found the sugar cubes and dried a spoon to go with them. The coffee began to whisper. I turned down the gas and opened the door of the refrigerator. It was completely empty except for a bottle of gin and half a carton of milk. I filled the cups and carried the tray into the bedroom.

'Wakey, wakey,' I said, sitting down on the edge of the bed.

Marjorie did not move.

'Hey. Good morning.'

She stirred slowly.

'What time is it?' she asked.

'It's rather early. It's a quarter past five,' I said.

She opened her eyes suddenly and lifted her head.

'Are you going?'

'I'm afraid I have to. Have some coffee. I made it for you.'

'Home to your wife?'

'Don't be so depressed about it.'

She sat up in bed and I put a pillow behind her so she could lean against the wall. She asked for her coffee black.

'I like your green coffee cups,' I said. 'They're French, aren't they?'

'I don't know. They were a house-warming present.'

We blew and sipped in silence.

'Come and lie here,' said Marjorie. She tapped the place in the bed where I had slept. I put down the tray and went round.

'You'll be more comfortable there,' she said, as I settled back. 'You don't really have to go? Do you?'

'I think I must.'

'We could have a nice time together.'

'I know that.'

159

'Then why don't you stay?'

'Just because I leave now doesn't mean that I disappear,' I said.

'Meaning?'

'I'm sure we'll see one another again.'

'I can be a wonderful woman you know. I just need a chance. I could bloom.'

I reached out and stroked her hand.

'You still wear your wedding ring,' I said.

She lifted her fourth finger and stared at the gold band set with a diamond.

'I tell my friends it won't come off. The joint's swollen. But I can get it off – easily. I just don't want to.'

Our fingers interlaced.

'It was very nice to be with you,' I said.

'It was human.'

We finished our coffee. It was getting lighter behind the curtains.

'I have to go,' I said. 'I've left a note for you on the glass table.'

'What sort? A "Dear John" '?

'No. It just says – oh well, you'll read it. It's brief.'

I got up and sat on the edge of the bed.

'What will you do today?' I asked.

'I have a friend,' she said, 'who has a dog. I shall probably take him for a walk on the Common, the dog I mean, a very, very long walk, and throw a lot of saliva-covered sticks for him to catch, and get very cross with him when he climbs out of a pond and shakes himself dry all over me.'

It was a cold summer's morning in the streets leading from Marjorie's with a grey overcast sky. I saw no one except for a solitary man in a raincoat exercising his dog. Wimbledon High Street was wide and strewn with papers which blew across my path like autumn leaves. Outside the station a single taxi now idled and bundles of newspapers lay in the entrance. In Ely's the lights were glowing and in one of the windows I noticed a red tent with a family of mannequins outside on camping chairs, grouped around a primus.

I turned on the radio. Sinatra singing 'New York New York' drifted from the speakers. I selected another station and heard: 'We're here on the route which the Royal couple will take to St Paul's and already it is thronged with thousands hoping to catch a glimpse of Charles and Diana when they pass. . . .'

It really was the day of the wedding. Eunice was off work as well and we would probably end up watching it on television. Holland Park, empty, seemed more attractive.

'. . . you, sir,' the commentator continued, 'would you like to tell me what part of Britain you've travelled from for this great occasion?'

'Limavady.'

'What part of Scotland is that, sir?'

'It's in County Londonderry.'

'Northern Ireland, of course. Now you madam . . . yes. . . ?' I turned it off. The common flashed by and I glimpsed stretches of scrubby grass, expanses of dark, stagnant water and sandy tracks. The road in front of me was shaded by trees. What exactly did I feel now that my great adventure was almost over? I expelled all thoughts so that I could concentrate on finding out. No sooner had I done so than the image entered my mind from a long-forgotten cartoon, of a man with a magnifying glass scrutinising a huge piece of abstract sculpture and asking, 'But what is it?' I banished the picture. Did I feel guilty? I waited in readiness but as far as I could tell I felt nothing. I thought back to the intimacy of the night before. Surely that would cause a reaction? I waited for the flutter in my stomach and the sensation of adrenalin beginning to stir. Again nothing.

My thoughts ran forward to the first moment when I would enter my house and smell the familiar odour of wax and peppermint in the hall, then to the moment when I would wake Eunice up, having changed into my pyjamas, and finally to the moment when she would ask me what I had done the night before. 'I came back and you had gone to bed,' I heard myself saying inwardly. This was what I had decided I would say. I had decided on it the previous evening, the split second after I had agreed to take Marjorie home. 'And did August have a nice evening?' I heard Eunice saying with my inner ear. 'Yes. August had a very nice evening,' I heard myself replying. Then I saw myself going downstairs, drinking the cold cream off the top of the milk bottle and putting the kettle on the stove. Everything was going to be as it had always been. Then I thought of our house, the rubber proof coats inside the front door, the smell of basil in the kitchen from the tiny pots above the sink, the sachets of lavender stitched into tiny pillow cases by Eunice which hung inside my cupboards. I could hardly wait to return to this warm, familiar world.

In the distance the windmill showed through a gap in the trees. My actions had reaped a reward. They had taught me to value what I had.

I imagine Marjorie stayed in bed drinking a second cup of coffee, read her book and dozed for a short while. When she woke up again she rolled over in the bed and smelt the pillow where August's head had been, inhaling the odour of his hair and his shampoo.

Later, when she read his note she felt annoyed. She read it cursorily, tore it up and threw it into the swing bin, where it settled amongst the damp granules from the previous night's coffee and quickly discoloured.

I reversed into a parking space near our house and climbed out. The sun was up and pools of light dappled the pavement. I locked the car door and tapped the handle to check that it was done. A transistor was playing and there was a smell of bacon. I looked up and down the street. Not a soul in sight.

I walked over to the garden gate, pushed it open and stepped through. The elm stretched above, while behind lay the house. Honeysuckle clung to the walls and I could smell it faintly. The gate banged shut behind me. I repeated to myself inwardly, 'Hello Eunice, I came back

162

late but you were already asleep.' It was then that I saw something dangling down from the letter box. I felt a tremor of anxiety.

I moved quickly forward and clambered up the steps. It was a piece of paper with my name written on it in Eunice's large and rounded writing. I pressed back the flap and pulled it out, then unfolded the paper.

> Dear August,
> I am fearful without you here. I have put the door on the chain. Ring the bell and I will come down and let you in. Ring hard and long as you know I'm a heavy sleeper.
> Love, Eunice

I folded it into quarters and slipped it into my breast pocket. This was not what I had planned. 'Hello Eunice', I heard myself saying inwardly, as I imagined her opening the door to me having removed the chain. 'Where were you last night?' I heard her responding. 'I went to the party,' I heard myself saying, 'and then we all went to a club. We stayed up all night and now here I am. . . .' On the doorstep I was at a disadvantage which I would not have been in her bedroom.

The key slipped easily into the latch and turned quietly. I eased the door back, the felt the tautness of the chain behind. I pulled the door to but without shutting it. It was no good worrying or trying to see a way around it. Unpleasant scenes were always best met head on.

The brass button of the bell was cold. Inside the house I could hear it pealing, a faint but anxious sound. I finished counting to ten and stepped back to wait.

The sound of Eunice's footfalls on the stairs was intimately known to me. It began as a faint flutter and gradually got louder. Footsteps on the parquet were more like tap-dancing heard at a distance. Of course Eunice would probably be bare-footed. That would be different again. More like a scudding.

I tilted my head back and looked up. There was no sound of any kind inside. Nor any sign of movement. I rang the bell again, this time counting to twenty. Once more the house replied with silence.

At the back of my throat it felt dry. I was rattled. I lifted up the brass letter flap and peered in. The row of coats, my mackintosh at the end, a small section of wallpapered wall, a corner of the parquet floor, was all that I could see.

'Hello?' I shouted. 'Hello . . . hello. . . .'

The spring of the letter flap hummed after it snapped shut. I rubbed my hand over my face, touching the raw stretches and the clumps of bristle.

The bell pealed a third time. I held it for thirty. Surely that would do it, I thought, as I held my ear to the door. But nothing stirred.

A minute later I hurried down the street and turned the corner. An old stooped man was standing in the doorway of the telephone kiosk. He was holding a piece of paper and looking at it carefully. A thick peeling white stick with rubber on the end swung from his arm. Despite the pain between my lungs I increased my pace. 'I have to make a telephone call – it's a matter of life and death,' I heard myself saying inwardly.

I skirted a pile of black plastic bags and crossed the road. The old man was leaning on his stick. He was staring at me through his spectacles. I stepped up onto the kerb. I was ten feet away from my objective. Suddenly he backed into the kiosk and wedged his stick so that it held the door open.

'Are you about to make a telephone call?' I heard myself asking.

'What?' replied the old man, in a high pitched, almost feminine voice.

'May I use the telephone?' I said. 'It's very important, I think my wife's had an accident.'

'My wife, yes,' said the old man, pronouncing the words with a smile.

'No, my wife. Can I use the phone?'

'I must phone my wife,' said the old man. 'But I need your help.'

This was ridiculous. I considered shouting or physically ejecting the old man, and then rejected both in turn.

'My wife, I must ring her now,' I stressed. I spoke as

if to a deaf man, elongating the words. 'Very important, matter of life and death.'

The old man was staring at me with his mouth open, showing two rows of porcelain false teeth. He was also nodding vigorously.

'Yes I must. It is very, very urgent,' said the old man.

'No, no. Not you – me!' I shouted. 'I must ring my wife.'

'I can't see the numbers. I'm almost blind.' The old man handed me the piece of paper he had been staring at. 'Will you dial it for me?'

'No. . . .'

'Thank you so much.'

I took the old man by the arm of his coat. I was going to pull him out of the kiosk. The old man stepped back making room for me.

'You're so kind,' he whispered, more feminine than ever. 'I have the money here.' A ten-pence piece lay on top of the grey box.

I began to dial the number brusquely. Damn him, damn him. How dare he be up and about and getting in my way at that time of the morning?

The ringing tone sounded at the other end. I violently thrust the receiver into the old man's bony hand. He looked at the apparatus but he did not move. He was like a character in a farce into whose hands a bomb has been thrust. I felt my anxiety and panic mounting. I was in a telephone kiosk, unable to call home because a lunatic happened to be in the queue before me, and now it transpired that the lunatic did not even know how to use the telephone.

I took the old man's arm and lifted it until the receiver was against the side of his head. It was then that I saw the flesh-coloured attachment jammed behind the ear. The old man was blind, but he was also deaf.

'Can you bloody hear?' I asked loudly.

The old man nodded although it was not clear whether it was to himself or me. The pips sounded. I pushed the ten pence into the slot. Chatter drifted from the mouthpiece.

'A nice man dialled the number for me,' whispered the old man in his thin female voice. 'Listen, I've only got ten pence. I can't find my travel pass. Will you go and look behind the fridge?'

I closed my eyes. The old man coughed quietly. A smell of urine and beer rose from the cement floor. I breathed the air coming through the open door.

'It's not there?' There was a note of panic in the old man's voice. 'What about on the shelf by the stove?'

I opened my eyes. 'Listen, please get a move on,' I shouted. The old man remained motionless.

I took him by the shoulder. 'Please hurry up. I must make my call immediately.' I drew my finger across my neck. 'Matter of life and death.'

The old man smiled behind his glasses, then he raised his hand like an adult signalling silence to an unruly child.

'Where?' said the old man. 'Under the pepper? Thank goodness. Well the pips are going. See you later, darling. No, you put the phone down first. Go on. Big kiss. . . .'

I took the receiver from the old man's grasp and slammed it down on the cradle.

'I must, *I must* make my call now.'

'Of course. Thank you very much. You've been very kind. What would I have done without you?'

I pushed the old man away out of the kiosk, handed him his stick and shut the door. At last, thank God. I drew ten pence out of my pocket and place it upright in readiness in the slot. I dialled my number rapidly. The familiar tone did not answer. I dialled again. The ringing started. Come on, come on, I urged. Get out of bed, Eunice. Answer the phone. But the ringing tone only repeated and repeated and repeated.

I dialled 100.

'Operator service,' said a matronly voice. 'Good morning.'

I gave the number and asked her to connect me. Again, the same story.

'There doesn't seem to be anyone there, caller,' said the operator finally. 'I suggest you try later. Goodbye.'

The line went dead. I put the telephone back on its cradle and went outside. When I saw the deaf old man was still there staring down at the pavement, I felt like hitting him.

'I can't get up the West End without my travel pass,'

the old man whispered. 'Today's the big day for Charles and Diana. I'll have to go home for it.'

'Oh, you stupid bore,' I muttered.

I sped across the road and ran past the plastic refuse bags. I did not stop running until I was inside my own gate. Now I was home what was I to do? I looked around wildly and my eyes lighted on the garden furniture listing on the corner. I didn't know if I would be able to but it would be worth a try.

I grasped the white metal table and began to drag it forward. The legs dug into the grass. My feet found the paving stones and I bumped it up over the stone lip. I continued backwards. The metal table legs scraped and gouged a line in the fine green slime.

I reached the house. In front of the basement window there was a well covered with bars. I wondered if I could stand the wrought-iron table on them and in turn stand on it to get to the living room window directly above. But the bars were too thin to balance the table legs on them.

I pushed the table into the space between the steps and the well. I clambered up. The table rocked unsteadily beneath me. I drew myself up to my full height. The living-room window was within reach but I was not close enough to gain entry.

I climbed down and went and fetched a garden chair. As I returned I noticed I was sweating across my back. I took off my jacket and threw it on the steps. Old leaves fell away from the seat as I lifted it up. I set it down on the table and gave the whole structure a rock. I would have to be very careful.

I climbed onto the table. My knees were shaking. I took two deep breaths and grasped the window ledge, put my foot on the chair and began to pull myself upwards. The structure swayed. My hand strained. I got my second foot on the chair and drew myself to my full height. I was in place.

I looked past the chintz curtains draped around the side of the window. There were the sofa and the armchairs arranged around the fireplace, the drums of pot pourri and the gold cage with the singing bird.

I gave the window a push and there was a slight movement. The hasp between the two halves of the sash was shut, as far as I could tell. There were also little cylinder locks which went through the wood of both sections. But in the summer, with the window being opened and shut so very often, these were rarely locked. The movement of the windows in their frame seemed to confirm this was so. At last something was going right.

I took my handkerchief out of my pocket and began to wrap it around my left knuckle. My left hand was weaker but it was closest to the pane which I was going to break. Using my teeth, for I was steadying myself with my right hand, I pulled the knot tight.

The glass shattered with the fourth blow. As it fell to the floor of the sitting room, I heard a voice behind.

'Excuse me sir, what are you doing?'

Remembering that I was very high and precariously balanced, I turned slowly.

It was a policeman standing by the garden gate, his hat tucked under his arm.

'I can't get in. I'm locked out. My wife is inside and I'm terribly worried,' I said in a rush.

'I'm sure we can do something to help you, sir,' said the policeman smiling. He came up to the table and looked up at me. 'Shall I help you down, sir?'

On the far side of the road I spotted Mrs Bradley standing in her front garden holding a smouldering frying pan.

'Who telephoned the police?' I asked.

'Even if knew I couldn't tell you, sir,' said the policeman. 'I just got the call on the radio and came here.'

Mrs Bradley saw that I was staring at her, dropped her arm with the frying pan, turned and ran back into her house.

'What did you say your name was?' the policeman enquired politely.

'Slemic.'

'Mr Slemic. Would you give me your hand? Thank you. Let your foot down. That's it.'

I felt better when my feet were back on the ground.

'Do you have any identification?' the policeman pressed.

'I live here,' I said sternly. 'My wife is inside. I'm terribly worried something has happened to her.'

'When did you last see Mrs Slemic?'

'Last night.'

The policeman was staring at me with a bemused and almost knowing expression.

'Have you had a domestic tiff, sir?' the policeman asked. 'Don't worry, we're pretty broadminded in the force. I mean, even I've been locked out by my wife.'

I picked up my jacket and pulled the note from the breast pocket.

'Read that,' I said. 'The front door's on the chain. That's why I can't get in.'

The policeman folded it open and began to read. I took my wallet out and extracted my driving licence. 'Look. That's me,' I said, forcing the transparent envelope into his hand.

'The door is chained. You're worried something has happened to Mrs Slemic?' said the policeman, returning the licence.

'That's right,' I said.

The policeman began to mount the steps. 'We'll have to see what we can do,' he said. He pushed back the door until the chain tightened behind. 'Doesn't look like it's very strong. Is it brass?'

'I can't remember. I think so,' I replied.

'I can force it if you like,' said the policeman. He was touching the chain with his thin fingers. 'Or I could radio for help?'

'Force it,' I said.

'Stand back, please.'

The policeman raised his booted foot and stamped very hard in the middle of the door. As a result of his exertion his hat slipped from his grip and rolled away down the steps. He stamped again, making a second dusty imprint in the paintwork beside the first. There was a screeching sound inside of metal tearing out of wood. He stamped a third time and the door swung back until it banged on the wall behind, causing a coat on the rack to fall to the floor like a corpse. I stepped forward.

'I'll go first if you don't mind, Mr Slemic,' said the policeman.

I saw he was barring my way with his arm.

'You follow me.'

169

The policeman stepped onto the mat and carefully wiped his feet. At the same time he held his head sideways. He was listening for something. He stepped away from me and headed for the corner. I stepped after him. Suddenly the policeman's expression changed from one of alertness to panic. He ran forward, disappearing from sight. I felt a great rush of adrenalin and at the same time a cold clear sense that the very worse had happened.

I came round the corner and saw the policeman was kneeling on the floor. He was crouching over a body. I ran forward until I could see over the blue serge shoulder. It was Eunice lying on the floor with her gollywog beside her. Her eyes were open and staring; her face was bruised; and her lips were dark, almost blue. The broken banister rail, the length of carpet torn from the stair rods and the unbroken bottle on the bottom step half-full of whisky told the rest of the story. Eunice had come down in the middle of the night for a drink and on her return she had slipped and fallen.

The policeman turned his head and looked up at me. 'I'm very sorry to have to tell you this, Mr Slemic,' he began. 'I'm afraid your wife must have an accident on the stairs. I'm afraid that she's dead.'

I ran out into the cloakroom and bent over the w.c. My vomit came out as a thin spear smelling of coffee and whisky and tears rolled down my cheeks.

Outside in the hall the policeman's walkie-talkie crackled into life.

Boxing Day 1981

We drove down a narrow tarmacadamed track through a sprawling graveyard to the Crematorium. It was an ugly, pseudo-classical building with fluted columns along the front. I had to be helped out of the hearse by the undertaker. He was a huge man in a black coat and pinstripe trousers and he carried a rolled-up umbrella. It was a boiling day and there was perspiration all over his upper lip which he kept wiping away.

Singing drifted from inside the building where a service was still going on. We stood waiting in a long silent line. There was my son Damian, his girlfriend Ruth, a nice-looking woman with big earrings who has subsequently become his fiancée, my partner David and his wife Karen with whom he had been reunited for the occasion, and Eunice's boss Mr Levy, a sad-faced old man with a lot of gold teeth. There was also a stranger who arrived separately. The stranger seemed to know Mr Levy, for he nodded to him grimly, but no one on our side knew him. I took this stranger to be one of those people who come to cremations or funerals because they have nothing better to do.

The mourners from the service before us filed out and began to climb into their cars. Everyone asked me if I was ready to go in. I leant on my son's arm and we went through the door. It was cold inside the chapel, like a larder. They had already brought Eunice's coffin in and it lay decked with flowers at the end. The clergyman came over and had a few words. I cannot remember what he said. We sat down on a pew at the front. The service began. The clergyman talked about death, not as an end but as a beginning. Eunice had not ended her existence: she had simply departed from this life and gone to a better place. I paid little attention to what he said but kept

171

staring at the coffin and trying to connect the woman I knew and the body lying inside the wood. I couldn't believe that Eunice was actually dead. I kept thinking it was a terrible nightmare from which I could wake up at any moment. I cried a great deal and I remember Ruth looking at me and squeezing my hand.

An aeroplane flew overhead, drowning the clergyman's voice. He had to stop and wait for it to pass. When he started again I recognised what he was saying. It was the ashes to ashes part, the words which can only be spoken at the moment of interment. In mid-sentence I saw the old clergyman was fumbling with a button at the side of his lectern and a second later the conveyor belt on which the coffin rested started to move. The wooden rollers made a great deal of noise as it bumped along. 'Dear Eunice,' I prayed. 'Please forgive me.' Then the coffin disappeared through the hole and the doors shut. The conveyor belt was turned off. I thought about the workmen behind the wall. The furnace would have been stoked and Eunice's coffin would soon be consigned to the flames.

The service was over. We went back outside into the heat. Mr Levy came over and hovered nervously. He asked if he had permission to introduce the stranger. I saw no reason why not. The stranger was called Mr Barnaby. (His first name was Charlie but I didn't know that then.) He was slightly pot-bellied with wavy silvery hair. We shook hands and he told me that he had known Eunice well. She had organised his finances. He was a client of Mr Levy's and he was connected with a small theatre somewhere in the Midlands. I told him how grateful I was that he had come. He replied that Eunice was more than a colleague, she was a friend, and with that we shook hands again and said goodbye. He didn't make much of an impression on me.

We climbed into the hearse. It had been standing in the sun and the seats were baking hot. As we drove back to the undertaker's I felt drunk, ecstatic, empty, desolate. I was a compound of every extreme emotion. That night I insisted on going back to our house. If I didn't face it then, empty and without Eunice, I knew I would never face it. Ruth insisted that she and Damian would keep me company and they slept together in the guest room. When I heard the faint noises of their love-making as I drifted towards sleep, I felt like laughing for the first time in days.

In the weeks immediately following the cremation I gave myself a set of tasks. I re-painted the spare bedroom. I found a man to tend the garden and even did a little work on it myself. I read some novels. I started cooking for myself. I felt sad and extremely lonely but never desperate. At night I had no difficulty falling asleep and I always woke up feeling untroubled.

Autumn came. The leaves began to turn and I started wearing a coat to work. One evening when I came home I found a set of black plastic bags lying on the doormat along with a plea that I give any old clothes which I might have to a charity for the hungry. I took it as the sign I had been waiting for.

It was a Saturday morning when I started. I had only been in Eunice's room once or twice since her death: now I was overwhelmed by it. The familiar smell of Eunice clung to everything. I began to pack and fold the dresses from her wardrobe. Soon my cheeks were wet. I told myself that it was an exorcism. I was letting out the grief as I had always known I would have to do.

In the afternoon I started on her chest of drawers. In the bottom where I know she kept her underwear, I was startled to find suspender belts, pairs of stockings and pieces of silk underwear which I had never known she had. Then I found a square black box from a West End department store. Inside the box, wrapped in tissue paper, there was a silk nightdress and a red garter and inside the garter there was a note. 'Darling One,' it began. 'The nightdress is the sacred part of this gift and the garter is the profane. I love you. Charlie B. the Bastard.' At the top the date was given as 'The Day Before the Royal Wedding Binge'. It wasn't long before I found the rest of the evidence underneath the lining paper of the drawer: dozens of letters and cards from one Charlie Barnaby. The name was familiar, but it was a few minutes before I

173

remembered. He was the stranger I had met after the cremation.

What did I learn from these letters? Their sex was adventurous and what he called 'naughty'. Eunice was 'the eel' or 'Jaws'. He was 'the tiger' or 'He who must be obeyed'. Once she came home after seeing him and found me already back, and had to take her stockings off in the street in case my suspicions were aroused. He wanted to marry but Eunice didn't want to leave me.

I could not say that my discoveries prompted them, for of course the grief and the despair were coming anyway. But they didn't help either. Two days afterwards, standing in the queue in the local supermarket, I burst into tears when the girl behind the till told me to move my basket. I was still crying when I got home. I felt like a receptacle from which tears could flow on for ever and I did not believe that my pain could ever be consoled. I turned to my doctor and he sent me to see a psychiatrist. The psychiatrist made me lie on a couch and describe what had happened. He didn't say much except that I had to 'work with my grief'. I didn't go back.

The days grew shorter and my soul grew darker. I took leave from the office and stayed at home. I did not want to see anyone. There was nowhere I wanted to go. I just wanted to nurse my grief, or to sit shouting abuse. I thought about selling the business but I was too depressed to write David a letter asking him if he wanted to buy it. I could see no reason for carrying on and I began thinking about suicide. I discovered that pills are best taken into a stomach full of jam. That holds them down when the body tries to sick them up.

Today is Boxing Day, the deadest day of my dead year. Ruth and Damian arrived early this morning. She was wearing a new dress which Damian had given her and a pair of shoes which she said were hurting her. David and his family arrived at one. He's back with his wife Midge of course and Karen is gone. So what's new? Even my clock-radio still needs tuning.

After lunch we pulled crackers, put on funny hats and played charades. I had to act out 'Everything You Always Wanted to Know About Sex But Were Afraid to Ask.' Then at five David and family went home in the Volvo.

I stacked the dishwasher. Damian and Ruth went back to his flat. They probably want to make love. They said something about telephoning here later.

I am alone now. I have been reading the entries I made exactly twelve months ago in the notebook Eunice gave me. Childhood traumas, a failed marriage, an unruly heir – it all adds up to a weary catalogue with no distinguishing features. I have Eunice's enormous bottle of Nembutal in front of me and a large glass of water. I have been imagining what I will do once I have taken them. I will put on my coat which I have lying on the sofa in readiness and I will go into the darkness outside. I will go down the road to the garden with the tombstone cemented to the wall: 'He was only a cat but he did his best'. The people who live in the house are away. Then I will curl up on the grass like a wild animal and in a couple of hours I will be gone. No one will find me until tomorrow at the earliest or the day after or perhaps, if I am very lucky, the day after that. And whoever discovers me will be a stranger.

Some nights ago I dreamt I was back in the cave among the stalagmites and stalactites. I made my way through the darkness to the pool where I had seen the fish without eyes. It was floating belly upwards and there was a faint smell of putrefaction. I have left no will. It will all go to Damian anyway.

The words which I have written down in this notebook, today and last year, will they be read like I have just read them, and will they be understood after I am dead? No doubt that is why I wrote them.

I have found myself on the brink but I cannot go ahead with it.

I am not only 'I' – I am August. I'm the man who wore a yellow paper hat in our charades. I'm the man whom Ruth told her shoes were hurting.

My life is mine, but to write it I can pretend it's someone else's.

Maybe what was meant by 'working with grief' was putting a shape to it and a form.

But how will I begin?

175

'I woke abruptly. The duvet was lying across my body and my feet were cold. I lifted the covers back over myself and wriggled my toes. I would lie there until they warmed up. High heels scuffed in the distance, like a needle on the centre of a record, then faded into silence. I thought of my journey to work through wooded streets; of the underground in the early morning haunted by smells of dust and perfume; and of women on the escalators in summer dresses with little red marks on the backs of their ankles where their shoes rubbed.'

I could give it until the end of the page.

Philip Reynolds (PhD FBPsS)
12, Hyde Park Mansions,
London, W2

17th May '82

Dear Mr Slemic,
                    Thank you for your manuscript
which I read with great interest. I cannot speak
of its literary qualities but only of its psychological
ones. I hope and imagine that what you have done
has eased your pain. Any work of this kind helps
to draw out the poison. I would also like to say
that I did mean you to take my words (when you
came to see me) as literally as you did. On the
other hand, perhaps they were the nudge which
you needed to start you 'scribbling' again? Your
description of your childhood writings made a
strong impression on me which has remained. I
hope that you will go on re-discovering those
powers of original thought.
    I enclose your manuscript.
                    With best wishes
                    Philip Reynolds

FOR THE BEST IN PAPERBACKS, LOOK FOR THE 🐧

In every corner of the world, on every subject under the sun, Penguin represents quality and variety – the very best in publishing today.

For complete information about books available from Penguin – including Pelicans, Puffins, Peregrines and Penguin Classics – and how to order them, write to us at the appropriate address below. Please note that for copyright reasons the selection of books varies from country to country.

In the United Kingdom: For a complete list of books available from Penguin in the U.K., please write to *Dept E.P., Penguin Books Ltd, Harmondsworth, Middlesex, UB7 0DA*

In the United States: For a complete list of books available from Penguin in the U.S., please write to *Dept BA, Penguin, 299 Murray Hill Parkway, East Rutherford, New Jersey 07073*

In Canada: For a complete list of books available from Penguin in Canada, please write to *Penguin Books Canada Ltd, 2801 John Street, Markham, Ontario L3R 1B4*

In Australia: For a complete list of books available from Penguin in Australia, please write to the *Marketing Department, Penguin Books Australia Ltd, P.O. Box 257, Ringwood, Victoria 3134*

In New Zealand: For a complete list of books available from Penguin in New Zealand, please write to the *Marketing Department, Penguin Books (NZ) Ltd, Private Bag, Takapuna, Auckland 9*

In India: For a complete list of books available from Penguin, please write to *Penguin Overseas Ltd, 706 Eros Apartments, 56 Nehru Place, New Delhi, 110019*

In Holland: For a complete list of books available from Penguin in Holland, please write to *Penguin Books Nederland B.V., Postbus 195, NL–1380AD Weesp, Netherlands*

In Germany: For a complete list of books available from Penguin, please write to *Penguin Books Ltd, Friedrichstrasse 10 – 12, D–6000 Frankfurt Main 1, Federal Republic of Germany*

In Spain: For a complete list of books available from Penguin in Spain, please write to *Longman Penguin España, Calle San Nicolas 15, E–28013 Madrid, Spain*

A CHOICE OF PENGUIN FICTION

Money Martin Amis

Savage, audacious and demonically witty – a story of urban excess. 'Terribly, terminally funny: laughter in the dark, if ever I heard it' – *Guardian*

Lolita Vladimir Nabokov

Shot through with Nabokov's mercurial wit, quicksilver prose and intoxicating sensuality, *Lolita* is one of the world's great love stories. 'A great book' – Dorothy Parker

Dinner at the Homesick Restaurant Anne Tyler

Through every family run memories which bind them together – in spite of everything. 'She is a witch. Witty, civilized, curious, with her radar ears and her quill pen dipped on one page in acid and on the next in orange liqueur . . . a wonderful writer' – John Leonard in *The New York Times*

Glitz Elmore Leonard

Underneath the Boardwalk, a lot of insects creep. But the creepiest of all was Teddy. 'After finishing *Glitz*, I went out to the bookstore and bought everything else of Elmore Leonard I could find' – Stephen King

The Battle of Pollocks Crossing J. L. Carr

Nominated for the Booker McConnell Prize, this is a moving, comic masterpiece. 'Wayward, ambiguous, eccentric . . . a fascinatingly outlandish novel' – *Guardian*

The Dreams of an Average Man Dyan Sheldon

Tony Rivera is lost. Sandy Grossman Rivera is leaving. And Maggie Kelly is giving up. In the steamy streets of summertime Manhattan, the refugees of the sixties generation wonder what went wrong. 'Satire, dramatic irony and feminist fun . . . lively, forceful and funny' – *Listener*

A CHOICE OF PENGUIN FICTION

Trade Wind   M. M. Kaye

An enthralling blend of history, adventure and romance from the author of the bestselling *The Far Pavilions*

The Ghost Writer   Philip Roth

Philip Roth's celebrated novel about a young writer who meets and falls in love with Anne Frank in New England – or so he thinks. 'Brilliant, witty and extremely elegant' – *Guardian*

Small World   David Lodge

Shortlisted for the 1984 Booker Prize, *Small World* brings back Philip Swallow and Maurice Zapp for a jet-propelled journey into hilarity. 'The most brilliant and also the funniest novel that he has written' – *London Review of Books*

Village Christmas   'Miss Read'

The village of Fairacre finds its peace disrupted by the arrival in its midst of the noisy, cheerful Emery family – and only the advent of a Christmas baby brings things back to normal. 'A sheer joy' – *Glasgow Evening Times*

Treasures of Time   Penelope Lively

Beautifully written, acutely observed, and filled with Penelope Lively's sharp but compassionate wit, *Treasures of Time* explores the relationship between the lives we live and the lives we think we live.

Absolute Beginners   Colin MacInnes

The first 'teenage' novel, the classic of youth and disenchantment, *Absolute Beginners* is part of MacInnes's famous London trilogy – and now a brilliant film. 'MacInnes caught it first – and best' – *Harpers and Queen*

A CHOICE OF PENGUIN FICTION

Stanley and the Women   Kingsley Amis

Just when Stanley Duke thinks it safe to sink into middle age, his son goes insane – and Stanley finds himself beset on all sides by women, each of whom seems to have an intimate acquaintance with madness. 'Very good, very powerful . . . beautifully written' – Anthony Burgess in the *Observer*

The Girls of Slender Means   Muriel Spark

A world and a war are winding up with a bang, and in what is left of London all the nice people are poor – and about to discover how different the new world will be. 'Britain's finest post-war novelist' – *The Times*

Him with His Foot in His Mouth   Saul Bellow

A collection of first-class short stories. 'If there is a better living writer of fiction, I'd very much like to know who he or she is' – *The Times*

Mother's Helper   Maureen Freely

A superbly biting and breathtakingly fluent attack on certain libertarian views, blending laughter, delight, rage and amazement, this is a novel you won't forget. 'A winner' – *The Times Literary Supplement*

Decline and Fall   Evelyn Waugh

A comic yet curiously touching account of an innocent plunged into the sham, brittle world of high society. Evelyn Waugh's first novel brought him immediate public acclaim and is still a classic of its kind.

Stars and Bars   William Boyd

Well-dressed, quite handsome, unfailingly polite and charming, who would guess that Henderson Dores, the innocent Englishman abroad in wicked America, has a guilty secret? 'Without doubt his best book so far . . . made me laugh out loud' – *The Times*

A CHOICE OF PENGUIN FICTION

Maia Richard Adams

The heroic romance of love and war in an ancient empire from one of our greatest storytellers. 'Enormous and powerful' – *Financial Times*

The Warning Bell Lynne Reid Banks

A wonderfully involving, truthful novel about the choices a woman must make in her life – and the price she must pay for ignoring the counsel of her own heart. 'Lynne Reid Banks knows how to get to her reader: this novel grips like Super Glue' – *Observer*

Doctor Slaughter Paul Theroux

Provocative and menacing – a brilliant dissection of lust, ambition and betrayal in 'civilized' London. 'Witty, chilly, exuberant, graphic' – *The Times Literary Supplement*

July's People Nadine Gordimer

Set in South Africa, this novel gives us an unforgettable look at the terrifying, tacit understanding and misunderstandings between blacks and whites. 'This is the best novel that Miss Gordimer has ever written' – Alan Paton in the *Saturday Review*

Wise Virgin A. N. Wilson

Giles Fox's work on the Pottle manuscript, a little-known thirteenth-century tract on virginity, leads him to some innovative research on the subject that takes even his breath away. 'A most elegant and chilling comedy' – *Observer* Books of the Year

Last Resorts Clare Boylan

Harriet loved Joe Fischer for his ordinariness – for his ordinary suits and hats, his ordinary money and his ordinary mind, even for his ordinary wife. 'An unmitigated delight' – *Time Out*

A CHOICE OF PENGUIN FICTION

Monsignor Quixote Graham Greene

Now filmed for television, Graham Greene's novel, like Cervantes' seventeenth-century classic, is a brilliant fable for its times. 'A deliciously funny novel' – *The Times*

The Dearest and the Best Leslie Thomas

In the spring of 1940 the spectre of war turned into grim reality – and for all the inhabitants of the historic villages of the New Forest it was the beginning of the most bizarre, funny and tragic episode of their lives. 'Excellent' – *Sunday Times*

Earthly Powers Anthony Burgess

Anthony Burgess's magnificent masterpiece, an enthralling, epic narrative spanning six decades and spotlighting some of the most vivid events and characters of our times. 'Enormous imagination and vitality . . . a huge book in every way' – Bernard Levin in the *Sunday Times*

The Penitent Isaac Bashevis Singer

From the Nobel Prize-winning author comes a powerful story of a man who has material wealth but feels spiritually impoverished. 'Singer . . . restates with dignity the spiritual aspirations and the cultural complexities of a lifetime, and it must be said that in doing so he gives the Evil One no quarter and precious little advantage' – Anita Brookner in the *Sunday Times*

Paradise Postponed John Mortimer

'Hats off to John Mortimer. He's done it again' – *Spectator*. A rumbustious, hilarious new novel from the creator of Rumpole, *Paradise Postponed* is now a major Thames Television series.

Animal Farm George Orwell

The classic political fable of the twentieth century.

FOR THE BEST IN PAPERBACKS, LOOK FOR THE

KING PENGUIN

A Confederacy of Dunces   John Kennedy Toole

In this Pulitzer-Prize-winning novel, in the bulky figure of Ignatius J. Reilly, an immortal comic character is born. 'I succumbed, stunned and seduced . . . it is a masterwork of comedy' – *The New York Times*

The Labyrinth of Solitude   Octavio Paz

Nine remarkable essays by Mexico's finest living poet: 'A profound and original book . . . with Lowry's *Under the Volcano* and Eisenstein's *Que Viva Mexico!*, *The Labyrinth of Solitude* completes the trinity of master-works about the spirit of modern Mexico' – *Sunday Times*

Falconer   John Cheever

Ezekiel Farragut, fratricide with a heroin habit, comes to Falconer Correctional Facility. His freedom is enclosed, his view curtailed by iron bars. But he is a man, none the less, and the vice, misery and degradation of prison change a man . . .

The Memory of War and Children in Exile: (Poems 1968–83)   James Fenton

'James Fenton is a poet I find myself again and again wanting to praise' – *Listener*. 'His assemblages bring with them tragedy, comedy, love of the world's variety, and the sadness of its moral blight' – *Observer*

The Bloody Chamber   Angela Carter

In tales that glitter and haunt – strange nuggets from a writer whose wayward pen spills forth stylish, erotic, nightmarish jewels of prose – the old fairy stories live and breathe again, subtly altered, subtly changed.

Cannibalism and the Common Law   A. W. Brian Simpson

In 1884 Tod Dudley and Edwin Stephens were sentenced to death for killing their shipmate in order to eat him. A. W. Brian Simpson unfolds the story of this macabre case in 'a marvellous rangy, atmospheric, complicated book . . . an irresistible blend of sensation and scholarship' – Jonathan Raban in the *Sunday Times*

FOR THE BEST IN PAPERBACKS, LOOK FOR THE

KING PENGUIN

Bedbugs Clive Sinclair

'Wildly erotic and weirdly plotted, the subconscious erupting violently into everyday life . . . It is not for the squeamish or the lazy. His stories work you hard; tease and torment and shock you' – *Financial Times*

The Awakening of George Darroch Robin Jenkins

An eloquent and powerful story of personal and political upheaval, the one inextricably linked with the other, written by one of Scotland's finest novelists.

In Custody Anita Desai

Deven, a lecturer in a small town in Northern India, is resigned to a life of mediocrity and empty dreams. When asked to interview the greatest poet of Delhi, Deven discovers a new kind of dignity, both for himself and his dreams.

Collected Poems Geoffrey Hill

'Among our finest poets, Geoffrey Hill is at present the most European – in his Latinity, in his dramatization of the Christian condition, in his political intensity . . . The commanding note is unmistakable' – George Steiner in the *Sunday Times*

Parallel Lives Phyllis Rose

In this study of five famous Victorian marriages, including that of John Ruskin and Effie Gray, Phyllis Rose probes our inherited myths and assumptions to make us look again at what we expect from our marriages.

Lamb Bernard MacLaverty

In the Borstal run by Brother Benedict, boys are taught a little of God and a lot of fear. Michael Lamb, one of the brothers, runs away and takes a small boy with him. As the outside world closes in around them, Michael is forced to an uncompromising solution.